THE SENIOR VICE PRESIDENT

JEFFREY ARCHER, whose novels and short stories include *Kane and Abel*, *A Prisoner of Birth* and *Cat O' Nine Tales*, has topped the bestseller lists around the world, with sales of over 270 million copies. He is the only author ever to have been a number one bestseller in fiction, short stories and non-fiction (*The Prison Diaries*). The author is married to Dame Mary Archer, and they have two sons, two grandsons and, at last, a granddaughter.

ALSO BY JEFFREY ARCHER

THE CLIFTON CHRONICLES
Only Time Will Tell   The Sins of the Father
Best Kept Secret   Be Careful What You Wish For
Mightier than the Sword   Cometh the Hour
This Was a Man

NOVELS
Not a Penny More, Not a Penny Less
Shall We Tell the President?   Kane & Abel
The Prodigal Daughter   First Among Equals
A Matter of Honour   As the Crow Flies
Honour Among Thieves
The Fourth Estate   The Eleventh Commandment
Sons of Fortune   False Impression
The Gospel According to Judas
(with the assistance of Professor Francis J. Moloney)
A Prisoner of Birth   Paths of Glory

SHORT STORIES
A Quiver Full of Arrows   A Twist in the Tale
Twelve Red Herrings   The Collected Short Stories
To Cut a Long Story Short   Cat O' Nine Tails
And Thereby Hangs a Tale

PLAYS
Beyond Reasonable Doubt   Exclusive   The Accused

PRISON DIARIES
Volume One – Belmarsh: Hell
Volume Two – Wayland: Purgatory
Volume Three – North Sea Camp: Heaven

SCREENPLAYS
Mallory: Walking Off the Map   False Impression

JEFFREY ARCHER

THE SENIOR
VICE PRESIDENT

PAN BOOKS

First published 2017 by Pan Books
an imprint of Pan Macmillan
20 New Wharf Road, London N1 9RR
Associated companies throughout the world
www.panmacmillan.com

ISBN 978-1-5098-6065-4

Visit **www.panmacmillan.com** to read more about all our books
and to buy them. You will also find features, author interviews and
news of any author events, and you can sign up for e-newsletters
so that you're always first to hear about our new releases.

To Cancer Research UK

FOREWORD

This year WHSmith celebrates its 225th anniversary, and to mark this momentous occasion we are pledging to raise £2 million to split between three charities: Cancer Research UK, Mind and the National Literacy Trust.

Several authors have kindly agreed to supply WHSmith with exclusive short stories in order to enable us to offer customers something new to the market and to donate £1 from each sale, split equally between the chosen charities.

We do hope you enjoy reading these specially chosen titles, and join us in thanking the authors for their support.

SANDRA BRADLEY
Trading Controller
Fiction Books

Dear Reader,

There are so many reasons I am delighted to support WHSmith's imaginative initiative to back three such worthwhile charities: Cancer Research UK, Mind and the National Literacy Trust.

Both my wife and I have suffered cancer in recent years, and thanks to the skill of two amazing doctors and their teams, aided by Cancer Research UK, we have both fully recovered.

I hope *The Senior Vice President* will amuse you but, far more important, the income will assist the three charities, which are so worthy of your support.

Thank you and best wishes,

Jeffrey Archer

THE SENIOR
VICE PRESIDENT

1

ARTHUR DUNBAR studied Mr S. Macpherson's account with some considerable satisfaction, bordering on pride. His eyes returned to the bottom line: $8,681,762. He checked it against last year's figure, $8,189,614. An increase of 6%, and one mustn't forget that during the past year his client had spent $281,601 on personal expenditure, which included all his household bills, and a quarterly payment to a Mr and Mrs Laidlaw, who, Arthur assumed, had to be his long-serving staff.

Arthur leant back in his chair, and not for the first time thought about the man who hailed from Ambrose in the Highlands of Scotland. When Arthur had first been given the responsibility of handling the account, some eighteen years ago, all his predecessor had told him was that a man, not much older than Arthur was at the time, had turned up at the bank and, having made a fortune on the railroad, deposited $871,000 in cash, and announced he was going home to Scotland.

It made Arthur smile to think that anyone who turned up with $10,000 in cash today would be subject to an investigation by their recently formed money-laundering team, and if they didn't tick all the boxes, their file was handed over to the Toronto Police's special investigation squad.

Arthur had long ago stopped trying to fathom why Mr Macpherson still did business with the National Bank of Toronto, when there were so many Scottish banks that were just as competent and considerably more convenient. But as he had conducted his affairs in an exemplary fash-ion for the past twenty-five years, the subject no longer arose, and in any case, NBT wouldn't have wanted to lose such an important customer.

Although Arthur knew very little about his client other than that they both shared the same heritage, one thing he had learnt over the years was that he was unquestionably a shrewd, intelligent businessman. After all, he had multi-plied his original investment tenfold, while at the same time withdrawing enough money to live an extremely comfortable lifestyle. In fact, only once in the past eight-een years had he failed to show a profit, despite stock market collapses, changes of governments and countless skirmishes around the globe. He appeared to have no vices, and his only extravagance was purchasing the occa-sional painting from Munro's, a fine art dealer in Edinburgh – and then only if it was by a Scottish artist.

Arthur had long ago accepted he didn't have Mr Macpherson's flair for finance, but he was quite happy to sit at the feet of the master and when any new instructions came, he would invest a portion of his own money in the same shares at a level no one would have noticed. So when the bank's senior vice president checked his own account at the end of the quarter, it stood at $243,519. How he would have liked to thank Mr Macpherson in person, because retirement was fast approaching for Arthur, and with his little nest egg and a full pension, he looked forward to ending his days in a degree of comfort he felt he had earned.

If there was a Mrs Macpherson there were no clues to suggest it, so Arthur rather assumed that, like him, his client was a bachelor. But like so many mysteries surrounding the man, he didn't know for sure, and assumed he never would.

However, something had been worrying Arthur about the account for the past few weeks, though he couldn't put a finger on it. He opened the file again and noted the figure, $8,681,762, before checking every entry meticulously. But all seemed to be in order.

He then studied each cheque that the different individuals and companies had presented during the past month, before checking them against the entry in the ledger. Every one tallied. All the usual household expenses and utility bills, food, wine, gas, electricity, even Hudsons, the local newsagent. But he still felt something wasn't quite right. And then, in the middle of the night, it hit him like a thunderbolt. Less, not more.

On arrival at the bank the following morning, the first

thing Arthur did was to take Mr Macpherson's ledger out of the bottom drawer. He turned the pages back to the previous quarter, and was able to confirm the most recent bills were considerably less than those for any other quarter. Had they been considerably more, Arthur would have spotted it immediately, and become suspicious. The fact that they were less, aroused his interest. The only entry that remained consistent was the monthly banker's order for his long-serving retainers, Mr and Mrs Laidlaw.

He leant back in his chair and wondered if he should inform the manager of this break in routine, but decided against it for two reasons. It was coming up to quarter day, when he would receive his new instructions from Mr Macpherson, and with it no doubt a simple explanation as to why the bills had fallen, and second, he didn't care much for the new manager of the bank.

There had been a time, not so very long ago, when Arthur had considered the possibility of being appointed manager himself, but his hopes were dashed when that position was filled by a Mr Stratton from their Montreal branch, who was half his age, but a graduate of McGill and the Wharton Business School. Arthur on the other hand had, to quote his late father, a former sergeant in the Seaforth Highlanders, risen through the ranks, and quite recently acquired the title of senior vice president. However, everyone in banking circles knew there were several vice presidents, and you only became the senior VP because everyone else had retired and you were next in line. 'Buggins' turn', as his father would have described it.

Arthur had applied to be the manager of one of the bank's smaller branches a couple of times, but hadn't even made the shortlist. On one occasion he'd overheard a member of the panel say, 'Dunbar's a good enough chap but simply isn't officer material.'

He had also considered leaving NBT to join one of their rivals, but quickly discovered he wouldn't be starting at the same salary, and he certainly couldn't hope to be offered the same pension plan as he was entitled to after so many years of loyal and devoted service. After all, in eighteen months' time he would have been with the bank for thirty years, which meant he could retire on two-thirds of his current salary; less than thirty years, and it would only be half. So he had to cling on for the next eighteen months.

Arthur turned his attention back to the pile of cheques on his desk, and was about to go over them once again, when the phone rang. He picked it up and immediately recognized the cheerful voice of Barbara, Mr Stratton's secretary.

'Mr Stratton wondered if you could pop round and see him when it's convenient –' code for as soon as possible – 'as there's something he'd like to discuss with you fairly urgently –' code for now.

'Of course,' said Arthur. 'I'll be with you in a moment.'

He disliked being summoned to the manager's office,

because it was rarely, if ever, good news. Last time Stratton had called for him was when he needed a volunteer to organize the Christmas party, and the responsibility had ended up taking hours of his spare time without any remuneration, and gone were the days when he could hope that one of the girls from the typing pool would go home with him later that evening.

The happiest of these occasions was when Barbara had joined the bank, and they had what might be described as a fling. He found they had so much in common, even enjoying the same passion for classical music, although he still couldn't understand why she preferred Brahms to Beethoven. And the biggest regret in Arthur's life was that he didn't ask her to marry him. When she married Reg Caldercroft in accounts, he ended up as best man.

He closed the Macpherson file and placed it in the top drawer of his desk, which he locked. He left his room and walked slowly down the corridor, knocked on the manager's door and received a curt 'Come' in response. Something else he didn't like about Mr Stratton.

Arthur opened the door and entered a large, well-furnished office, and waited to be told he could sit down. Stratton smiled up at him and pointed to the chair on the other side of his desk. Arthur returned the smile, equally insincere, wondering what voluntary chore was about to be thrust upon him.

'Good morning, Arthur,' said the young man.

'Good morning, Mr Stratton,' replied Arthur, who had

once addressed him as Gerald when he first took over as manager, only to be told, 'not during working hours'. And as they never met socially, it was also the last time he had addressed the manager by his Christian name.

'Arthur,' he said, the same smile. 'I've had a letter from head office that I felt I ought to share with you, remembering that you are the bank's senior vice president and our longest-serving member of staff.'

What's he after? was Arthur's first thought.

'I have been instructed to make cutbacks on staff. The figure they are insisting on,' Stratton said, looking down at a letter on his desk, 'is ten per cent. And the board are recommending we start by offering senior staff the opportunity to take early retirement.'

To make way for younger people who they will only have to pay half the salary, Arthur wanted to say, but kept his counsel.

'And of course, I thought you might consider this an ideal opportunity, after your little scare last year.'

'It wasn't a scare,' said Arthur, 'and I was off work for four days. The only four days in nearly thirty years with the bank,' he reminded Stratton.

'Indeed, most commendable,' said Stratton. 'But don't you think these things are sometimes a warning?'

'No, I do not,' said Arthur. 'I've never felt fitter, and as you well know, I only need to serve another eighteen months to qualify for a full pension.'

'I realize that,' said Stratton, 'and please don't think

I'm not sympathetic. But my hands are tied.' He looked down at the letter, clearly trying to place the blame on someone else. 'I'm sure you'll appreciate the problem I'm facing . . .'

'It's me who's facing the problem, not you,' said Arthur, bolder than he'd ever been in the past.

'And the board asked me to say,' said Stratton, 'how much they appreciate the long and dedicated service you have given the bank. And I feel sure you'll be pleased to know they have agreed that a farewell party should be thrown in your honour, along with an appropriate gift to mark your remarkable service to the National Bank of Toronto.'

'A cocktail party with crisps, peanuts, a glass of *vin ordinaire*, and a gold-plated watch. Thanks very much. But I'd rather have the full pension I'm entitled to.'

'And I want you to know, Arthur,' said Stratton, ignoring the outburst, 'how hard I fought your corner, but the board . . . well, I feel sure you know what they're like.'

Actually Arthur didn't have any idea what they were like. In fact if a member of the board had passed him in the street, he doubted if they would recognize him.

'But I did manage one small coup on your behalf,' continued Stratton, the same insincere smile returning to his face. 'I got you a stay of execution.' And from the look on the manager's face, he clearly regretted the words the moment he'd uttered them, but it didn't stop him charging on. 'While everyone else will have to leave by the end of the next quarter, six months at the most, you can retain your position as the senior VP for another year.'

'Just six months before I would have scraped over the line,' said Arthur with considerable feeling.

'I did the best I could given the circumstances,' insisted Stratton. 'And will be writing to you in the next few days, setting out the finer details.' The manager hesitated for a moment before adding, 'I was rather hoping, Arthur, I might rely on you to brief other senior colleagues of the board's decision. You're so good at that sort of thing.'

Arthur rose from his place with as much dignity as he could muster, and said calmly, 'Go to hell, Gerald. You can do your own dirty work for a change.' He gave the manager the same ingratiating smile, and left without another word.

Once Arthur was back in his office, he swore out loud, something he hadn't done since the Toronto Maple Leafs lost to the Montreal Canadiens during the last minute of extra time in the Stanley Cup.

He paced aimlessly around his little office for some time before he finally sat down and began to write a letter to Mr Macpherson explaining why someone else would be handling his account in the future.

◄◦►

A fortnight passed, but there was no reply from Ambrose Hall. This surprised Arthur, because if there was one thing that he knew about his most esteemed customer, he was never less than courteous and unfailingly punctilious.

The bank's senior VP continued to double-check his mail every morning, but there was still no response to his letter. Even more out of character, when quarter day appeared on the calendar, the usual long letter detailing Mr Macpherson's investment instructions and any other requirements he expected the bank to carry out during the next three months did not appear.

It was while Arthur was trying to get to sleep that the only other possibility for Mr Macpherson's unaccountable silence crossed Arthur's mind. He sat bolt upright and didn't sleep again that night.

Nevertheless, it was still another fortnight before Arthur would accept that the 'only other possibility', had become a probability. But it wasn't until he'd opened a letter from Mr Stratton confirming the day of his retirement and his pension details, that the first dishonest thought crossed Arthur Dunbar's mind in twenty-eight years of service to the National Bank of Toronto.

However, Arthur was, by nature, a cautious man, who in the past had always played the long game, so he allowed the dishonest thought to nurture for a while before he even considered a provisional plan – in his mind.

During the following month, he continued to clear every cheque that was presented in his client's name, as well as Mr and Mrs Laidlaw's monthly banker's order deposited to their joint account at the Bank of Scotland in

Ambrose. However, when a new chequebook arrived from the printers, Arthur did not send it on to Mr Macpherson, but locked it in the top drawer of his desk.

He felt confident that would elicit an immediate response if . . .

The one letter that *did* land on his desk was hand delivered by Mr Stratton's secretary, and was short and to the point.

It is with much regret . . .

Nowhere in the letter were the words 'sacked' or 'made redundant', because they had been replaced with wishing him a happy retirement, and how much he was looking forward to continuing working with him for the next ten months. Arthur swore for the second time.

The rest of the month passed without incident, although no letter was forthcoming from Mr Macpherson. The staff party was considered a great success by everyone except Arthur, who was the last to leave, and spent Christmas alone.

‑‹o›‑

Arthur checked his calendar: 7 January, and he still hadn't received any further communication from Mr Macpherson, although he was aware any payments would soon come to an end, because he hadn't issued a new chequebook for the past quarter. But then Arthur was in no hurry, because he still had another nine months to work on his exit strategy, as befitted a banker who believed in the long game.

When no instructions came from Mr Macpherson by the end of the following quarter, Arthur decided he must either be too ill to communicate, or he was dead. He considered his next move very carefully. He thought about writing to Mr Macpherson concerning a recent dividend he'd received from the Shell Oil Company, asking if he wanted to accept payment, or to take up their offer of new shares. After considerable thought, he didn't send the letter, as he feared it might alert Mr and Mrs Laidlaw to the fact that someone at the bank was becoming suspicious.

Arthur decided he would wait for the cheques to run out before he made his next move, and every time a new chequebook arrived from the printers, he placed it in his top drawer along with the others.

Patience paid off, because the Laidlaws finally gave themselves away. When the last four cheques were sent to be cleared, Arthur noted that the sums were becoming larger and larger, and he made an arbitrary decision that, despite the account still having over eight million dollars in cash, stocks and bonds, he would return the final cheque made out for British Airways to a travel company in Edinburgh. He waited for an irate call from Mr and Mrs Laidlaw, possibly even one from Mr Macpherson, but none was forthcoming, which gave Arthur the confidence to put the second part of his plan into action.

2

WHENEVER ANYONE asked Arthur where he was going for his summer holiday, and not many people did, he always replied, 'I will be visiting my sister in Vancouver.' However, by the time it came for him to leave for his summer vacation, he not only had a sister, but a whole family in place: Eileen and Mike who worked in local government, and a niece and nephew, Sue and Mike Jr, not very imaginative, but when you haven't lied for twenty-nine years, your friends and colleagues have a tendency to believe everything you tell them.

During the next month, Arthur continued to invest Mr Macpherson's fortune in an orderly, if somewhat conservative fashion, keeping to a well-trodden path. At the same time, he withdrew small amounts of cash each week from his personal account, until he had a little over three thousand dollars locked away in his top drawer, not unlike a bridegroom preparing for his wedding.

On the Monday morning a week before he was due to go on holiday, Arthur placed the cash in his lunch box and headed off for his favourite bench in the park. However, on the way he dropped into the Royal Bank of Canada, where he waited in line at the currency counter, before changing his dollars into pounds.

During the Tuesday lunchbreak, he made a further detour, to a local travel agent, where he purchased a return flight to Vancouver. He paid by cheque, and when he arrived back at the bank, left the ticket on the corner of his desk for all to see, and if anyone mentioned it, he once again told them all about his sister Eileen and her family in Vancouver.

On the Wednesday, Arthur applied for a new credit card on Mr Macpherson's behalf, and issued an order to cease any trading on the old one. A bright, shiny black card appeared on his desk forty-eight hours later. Arthur was ready to carry out stage two of his plan.

He had carefully selected the dates he would be away from the office, choosing the two weeks before Mr Stratton was due to take his annual leave.

Arthur left the bank just after six on Friday evening, and took the usual bus back to his small apartment in Forest Hill. He spent a sleepless night wondering if he'd made the right decision. However, by the time the sun eventually rose on Saturday morning, he was resolved to go ahead with his plan and, as his father would have said, 'let the devil take the hindmost'.

After a leisurely breakfast, he packed a suitcase and left the flat just before midday. Arthur hailed a cab, an expense he normally wouldn't have considered, but then in a few months' time he would be either a multimillionaire living in Ambrose Hall, or spending his retirement in a prison cell.

When the cab dropped him off at the domestic terminal, Arthur went straight to the Air Canada desk and traded in his return flight to Vancouver for a one-way window seat at the back of a plane destined for London. He paid the difference in cash. Arthur then took the shuttle bus across to the international terminal, where he was among the first to check in. While he waited to board the aircraft, he sat behind a large pillar and, head down, read the *Toronto Star*. He intended to be among the first on, and the last off the plane, as he hoped it would cut down the chances of anyone recognizing him.

Once he'd fastened his seat belt, he made no attempt to strike up a conversation with the young couple seated next to him. During the seven-hour flight, he watched two films, which he wouldn't have bothered with back at home, and in between pretended to be asleep.

When the plane touched down at Heathrow on Sunday morning, he waited patiently in line at Immigration, and by the time his passport had been stamped, his one suitcase was already circling around on the baggage carousel. Once he'd cleared Customs, he took another shuttle bus to terminal five, where he purchased a ticket to Edinburgh, which he also paid for in cash. On arrival, another taxi took him to the Caledonian, a hotel recommended by the cabbie.

'How long will you be staying with us, Mr Macpherson?' asked the receptionist.

'Just a couple of nights,' replied Arthur, as she handed him his room key.

Arthur feared he'd have another sleepless night, but in fact fell into a deep sleep within moments of putting his head on the pillow.

—◦—

The following morning, he ordered breakfast in bed, another first. But the moment he heard nine chiming on a nearby clock, he picked up the phone on his bedside table and dialled a number he did not have to look up.

'Royal Bank of Scotland, how can I help you?'

'I'd like to speak to the senior accounts manager,' said Arthur.

'Buchan,' said the next voice that came on the line. 'How can I help you?'

'I'm thinking of moving my account to your bank,' said Arthur, 'and wondered if I could make an appointment to see you.'

'Of course,' said a voice suddenly sounding more conciliatory. 'Would eleven tomorrow morning suit you, Mr . . . ?'

'Macpherson,' said Arthur. 'Yes, that would be just fine.'

—◦—

Jet lag caused Arthur to oversleep, so he skipped breakfast and, following the doorman's instructions, made his way down Princes Street, occasionally stopping to window shop, as he didn't want to be early for his appointment.

He entered the bank at 10.55 a.m., and a receptionist accompanied him to Mr Buchan's office. The senior accounts manager rose from behind his desk and the two men shook hands.

'How can I help you, Mr Macpherson?' Buchan asked once his potential new client had sat down.

'I'll be moving back to Scotland in a few months' time, and your bank was recommended to me by the senior vice president at NBT.'

'Our partner bank in Toronto,' said Buchan, as he opened a drawer in his desk and extracted some forms.

For the next twenty minutes, Arthur answered a series of questions that he was in the habit of asking. Once the last box had been filled in, and Arthur had signed *S. Macpherson* on the dotted line, Buchan asked if he had any form of identity with him, such as a passport.

'I'm so sorry,' said Arthur, 'I left my passport at the Caledonian. But I do have my credit card.'

The production of a platinum credit card seemed to be more than enough to satisfy the account manager.

'Thank you,' said Buchan, as he handed back the card. 'And may I ask when you expect the transfer to take place?'

'Sometime in the next few weeks,' replied Arthur, 'but

I will ask Mr Dunbar, the bank's senior vice president, who has handled my account for the past twenty years, to give you a call.'

'Thank you,' said Buchan. 'I look forward to hearing from him.'

Arthur walked slowly back to the hotel feeling the meeting couldn't have gone much better. He collected his case from his room, and returned to reception.

'I hope you enjoyed your stay with us, Mr Macpherson,' said the receptionist, 'and it won't be too long before we see you again.'

'I hope so too,' said Arthur, who settled his bill in cash, left the hotel, and asked the doorman to hail a taxi.

When he was dropped off at the station, a journey he would normally have walked, Arthur joined another queue, and purchased a first-class return ticket to Ambrose. He sat alone in a comfortable carriage watching the countryside race by as the train travelled deeper and deeper into the Highlands, skirting several lochs and foreboding pine forests, while he went over the finer details of the most crucial part of his plan.

To date, everything had run smoothly, but he had long ago accepted the real hurdle that still needed to be crossed would be when he came face to face with Mr and Mrs Laidlaw for the first time.

On arrival in Ambrose, Arthur climbed into the back of another taxi, and asked the driver to take him to the best hotel in town. This was greeted with a chuckle, and,

'You've obviously never visited these parts before. You have two choices, the Bell Inn or the Bell Inn.'

Arthur laughed. 'Well then, that's settled. And can I also book you for ten o'clock tomorrow morning?'

'Yes, sir,' said the driver cheerfully. 'Would you prefer this car, or I have a limousine?'

'The limousine,' said Arthur, without hesitation. He needed the Laidlaws to realize who they were dealing with.

'And where will we be going?' he asked, as they drew up outside the Bell Inn.

'Ambrose Hall.'

The driver turned and gave his fare a second look, but said nothing.

Arthur walked into the pub, where the bar doubled as the reception desk. He booked a room for the night, and told the landlord he couldn't be certain how long he would be staying, not adding, because if the front door of Ambrose Hall was opened by Mr Macpherson, he'd be on the next flight back to Toronto.

Once Arthur had unpacked, taken a bath and changed his clothes, he made his way back downstairs to the bar. The few locals stared at him disapprovingly, assuming he was an Englishman, until he opened his mouth, when their smiles returned.

He ordered cock-a-leekie soup and a Scotch egg, delighted to find that although the regulars continued to view him with suspicion, the landlord seemed quite happy to chat, especially if it was accompanied by the offer of a wee dram.

During the next hour and after nearly emptying a bottle of wee drams, Arthur discovered that no one in the town had ever met Mr Macpherson, although, the landlord added, 'the shopkeepers have no complaints, because the man always pays his bills on time and supports several local charities' – which Arthur could have listed. He noted the words 'pays' and 'supports', so certainly the landlord thought Macpherson was still alive.

'Came over from Canada in my father's day,' continued the barman. 'Said to have made a fortune on the railroad, but who knows the truth?'

Arthur knew the truth.

'Must be lonely up there in the winter,' said Arthur, still fishing.

'And the ice rarely melts on those hills before March. Still, the old man's got the Laidlaws to take care of him, and she's a damned fine cook, even if he's not the most sociable of people, especially if you stray onto his land uninvited.'

'I think I'll turn in,' said Arthur.

'Care for a nightcap?' asked the landlord, holding up an unopened bottle of whisky.

'No, thank you,' said Arthur.

The landlord looked disappointed, but bade his guest goodnight.

Arthur didn't sleep well, and it wasn't just jet lag: after

the barman's remarks he feared Macpherson might still be alive, in which case the whole trip would have been a complete waste of time and money. And worse, if Stratton got to hear about it . . .

◄◦►

When the sun rose the following morning, which Arthur noted was quite late in this part of the world, he took a bath, got dressed and went downstairs to enjoy a breakfast that would have been appreciated in New York: porridge with brown sugar, kippers, toast, marmalade and steaming hot coffee. He then returned to his room and packed his small suitcase, still not certain where he would be spending the night.

He came back downstairs and, on being handed his bill, discovered just how many wee drams the landlord had enjoyed. But this was not somewhere to hand over a credit card in the name of Mr S. Macpherson. That remained in his wallet. For now, its only purpose had been to prove his identity to Mr Buchan. Arthur settled the bill with cash, which brought an even bigger smile to the landlord's face.

When Arthur stepped out of the hotel just before ten o'clock, he was greeted with the sight of a gleaming black Daimler.

'Good morning,' he said, as he climbed into the back seat and sank down into the comfortable leather upholstery.

'Good morning, sir,' said the driver. 'Hope the car's to your liking.'

'Couldn't be better,' replied Arthur.

'Usually only comes out for weddings or funerals,' admitted the driver.

Arthur still wasn't sure which this was going to be.

The driver set off on the journey to Ambrose Hall, and it quickly became clear he hadn't visited the house for some time, and like everyone else in the town, had never set eyes on Mr Macpherson, but he added with a chuckle, 'They'll have to call for Jock when the old man dies.'

The hall turned out to be a journey of about fourteen miles, during which the roads became lanes, and the lanes, paths, until he finally saw a turreted castle standing four-square on a hill in the distance. Arthur had one speech ready, should Mr Macpherson answer the door, and an-other if he was met by the Laidlaws.

The car proceeded slowly up the driveway, and they must have been about a hundred yards from the front door when Arthur saw him. A massive giant of a man wearing a kilt, with a cocked shotgun under his right arm, looking as if he hoped a stag might stray across his path.

'That's Hamish Laidlaw,' said Jock, 'and if you don't mind, I think I'll stay in the car.'

When Arthur got out, he heard the car doors lock. He began walking slowly towards his prey.

'What di ye want?' demanded Laidlaw, his gun rising a couple of inches.

'I've come to see Mr Macpherson,' said Arthur, as if he was expected.

'Mr Macpherson doesn't welcome strangers, especially those who dinnae have an appointment,' he said, the gun rising a couple more inches.

'He'll want to see me,' said Arthur, who took out his wallet, extracted a card, and handed it to the giant. Arthur suspected this might be one of those rare occasions when senior vice president embossed in gold below National Bank of Toronto might just have the desired effect.

While Laidlaw studied the card, Arthur watched as a moment of apprehension crossed his face, a look he'd experienced many times when a customer was asking for an overdraft, and didn't have the necessary security to back it up. The shift of power had changed, and Arthur knew it.

'He's not here at the moment,' said Laidlaw, as the gun dropped.

'I know he isn't,' said Arthur, taking a risk, 'but if you don't want the whole town to know why I've come to visit you,' he added, looking back at Jock, 'I suggest we go inside.' He began walking slowly towards the front door.

Laidlaw got there just in time to open it, and led the intruder into the drawing room, where all the furniture was covered in dust sheets. Arthur pulled one off and let it fall to the floor. He sat down in a comfortable leather chair, looked up at Laidlaw and said firmly, 'Fetch Mrs Laidlaw. I need to speak to both of you.'

'She wasn't involved,' said Laidlaw, fear replacing bluster.

Involved in what? thought Arthur, but repeated, 'Fetch your wife. And while you're at it, Laidlaw, put that gun away, unless you want to add murder to your other crimes.'

Laidlaw scurried away, leaving Arthur to enjoy the magnificent paintings by Mackintosh, Farquharson and Peploe that hung from every wall. Laidlaw reappeared a few minutes later with a middle-aged woman in tow. She was wearing an apron, and didn't raise her head. It wasn't until she stopped half a pace behind her husband that Arthur realized just how much she was shaking.

'I know exactly what you two have been up to,' said Arthur, hoping they would believe him, 'and if you tell me the truth, and I mean the whole truth, there's just a chance I might still be able to help you. If you don't, my next visit will be to the local police station. I'll start with you, Mrs Laidlaw.'

'We didnae mean to do it,' she said, 'but he didn't leave us with a lot of choice.'

'Hold your tongue, woman,' said Laidlaw. 'I'll speak for both of us.'

'You'll do nothing of the sort,' said Arthur. He looked back at Mrs Laidlaw and played what he hoped was his trump card. 'The first thing I want to know is when Mr Macpherson died?'

'Just a few months back,' said Mrs Laidlaw. 'I found

him in bed, white as a sheet he was, so he must have passed away during the night.'

'Then why didn't you call for a doctor, the police, even Jock?'

'Because we didn't think straight.' She paused. 'We thought we'd lose our jobs and be turfed out of the lodge. So we waited to see what would happen if we did nothing, and as the monthly cheque kept arriving from the bank, we assumed no one could be any the wiser.'

'What did you do with the body?'

'We buried him. On the other side of the copse,' chipped in Mr Laidlaw, 'where no one would find him.'

'We didn't mean any harm,' she said, 'but we'd served the laird for over twenty years, and not so much as a pension.'

I know the feeling, thought Arthur, but didn't interrupt.

'We didn't steal nothing,' said Laidlaw.

'But you signed cheques in his name, and also went on receiving your monthly pay packet.'

'Only enough to keep us alive, and not allow the house to go to rack and ruin.'

'I told him we had to keep the expenses low,' said Mrs Laidlaw, 'so they wouldn't become suspicious.'

'That's what gave you away,' said Arthur.

'Will we go to jail?' asked Mrs Laidlaw.

'Not if you carry out my instructions to the letter,' said Arthur as he stood up. 'Is that understood?'

'I don't care about going to jail,' said Laidlaw, 'but not Morag. It wasn't her fault.'

'I'm afraid you're both in this together,' said Arthur. Mrs Laidlaw began to shake again. 'Now I want to see Mr Macpherson's study.'

The Laidlaws both looked surprised by the request, but quickly led Arthur out of the drawing room and up a wide sweeping staircase to a large comfortable room on the first floor that had been converted to an office.

Arthur walked across to a desk that overlooked the hills of Arbroath. He was surprised to find not a speck of dust on the furniture, only perpetuating the myth that their master was still alive. The Laidlaws stood a few paces back, as their unwelcome visitor sat down at the desk. A flicker of a smile crossed Arthur's lips when he spotted the Remington Imperial typewriter on which Mr Macpherson had written so many letters to him over the years.

'Would you like a cup of tea, sir?' asked Mrs Laidlaw, as if she were addressing the master of the house.

'That would be nice, Morag,' said Arthur. 'Milk and one sugar, please.'

She disappeared, leaving her husband almost standing to attention. Arthur opened the top drawer of the desk to find a stack of used chequebooks, the stubs filled in with Macpherson's familiar neat hand. He closed the drawer and took out a piece of Ambrose Hall headed notepaper, and slipped it into the typewriter.

Arthur began to write a letter to himself, and after he'd typed 'Yours sincerely', he pulled the page out and read it, before turning to Laidlaw. 'I want you to read this letter carefully and then sign it.'

Laidlaw couldn't hide his surprise long before he finished reading the letter. But he took the quill pen from its holder, dipped it in the black ink and slowly wrote 'S. Macpherson'. Arthur was impressed, and wondered how long it had taken Laidlaw to perfect the forgery, because he'd never spotted it. He took an envelope from the letter rack, placed it in the machine and typed:

Mr A. Dunbar
Senior Vice President
The National Bank of Toronto

He placed the letter in the envelope and sealed it, as Mrs Laidlaw returned carrying a tray of tea and shortbread biscuits. Arthur took a sip. Just perfect. He placed the cup back on its saucer and set about writing a second letter. When he had finished, he asked Laidlaw to once again add the false signature, but this time he didn't allow him to read the contents.

'Post one today,' said Arthur. 'And this one a week later,' he added, before passing both envelopes across to Laidlaw. 'If the second letter arrives on my desk within a fortnight, I shall return in a few weeks' time. If it doesn't your next visitor will be a police officer.'

'But how will we survive while you're away?' asked Laidlaw.

Arthur opened his briefcase and took out three chequebooks. 'Use them sparingly,' he said, 'because if I consider you have overstepped the mark, the cheque will not be cleared. Is that understood?' They both nodded. 'And you'll also need to order some more writing paper and envelopes,' continued Arthur, as he opened the drawer. 'And stamps.'

Arthur was just about to close the drawer when he spotted some documents tucked away in a corner. He pulled out Mr Macpherson's old passport, his birth certificate, and a will, and could feel his heart hammering in his chest. The three finds also supplied a wealth of information that might prove useful in the future, and he finally discovered what the S. stood for. Macpherson's passport also revealed that he was sixteen years older than Arthur, but given the blurriness of the old photograph he felt he could get away with it. But he would still need to order a replacement before he returned to Toronto. He placed the passport, birth certificate and the will in his briefcase and locked it. He stood up and began to walk towards the door. The Laidlaws followed obediently in his wake.

'Mrs Laidlaw, I want all the dust sheets removed, and the house returned to the state it was in when Mr Macpherson was still in residence. Spare no expense, just be certain to send me every bill, so I can double-check it,' he added, as they walked downstairs together.

'By the time you return, Mr Dunbar, everything will be just as you would expect it,' she promised.

'As Mr Macpherson would expect it,' Arthur corrected her.

'Mr Macpherson,' she said. 'I'll prepare the master bedroom so it will be just like old times.'

'Is there anything else you'd like me to do, sir?' asked Laidlaw when Arthur reached the bottom of the staircase.

'Just be sure to post those two letters, and carry on as if Mr Macpherson was still alive, because he is,' said Arthur, as Laidlaw opened the front door.

When Jock saw them coming out of the house with Hamish Laidlaw clutching on to his hat, and no longer holding a gun, he jumped out of the car, ran around and opened the back door so Arthur could climb in.

'Where to, sir?' said Jock.

'The station,' Arthur said, as he looked out of the window to acknowledge the Laidlaws waving, as if he were already the master of Ambrose Hall.

◄○►

During the flight back to Heathrow, Arthur studied Mr Macpherson's last will and testament line by line. He had left generous legacies to the Laidlaws, while no other individual was mentioned. The bulk of the estate was to be divided between several local organizations and charities, the two largest amounts being allocated to the Scottish

Widows and Orphans Fund, and the Rehabilitation of Young Offenders Trust. Did those simple bequests, Arthur wondered, explain why the young Scot had set sail for Canada, and ended his days as a recluse in a remote part of his homeland?

Arthur knew the passport and birth certificate could prove useful if he was to go ahead with the deception, but had already decided that when he died, the executors would find the will exactly where Mr Macpherson had left it.

On arrival back at Heathrow, Arthur took a train to Paddington and a taxi on to Petty France. Once he'd entered the building, he spent some considerable time filling in a long form, something he was rather good at.

After double-checking every box, he joined a slow-moving queue, and when he eventually reached the front he handed the document to a young lady seated behind the counter. She studied the application carefully, before asking to see Mr Macpherson's old passport, which Arthur handed over immediately. He'd made only one subtle change, 1950 had become 1966, while his own photograph was attached to the application. She was clearly surprised not to have to make any corrections on his application form, or ask for further information. She smiled up at Mr Macpherson and stamped APPROVED.

'If you come back tomorrow afternoon, Mr Macpherson,' she said, 'you'll be able to pick up your new passport.'

Arthur thought about making a fuss as he had a flight

booked for Toronto that night, but simply said, 'Thank you,' as he didn't want to be remembered.

Arthur checked into the nearest hotel, where he spotted a poster advertising a performance of Schubert's Fifth, to be given at the Festival Hall by the Berlin Philharmonic under their conductor, Simon Rattle.

He was beginning to think the trip couldn't have gone much better.

3

ARTHUR PICKED UP the phone on his desk and pressed a button that would put him through to the manager's office.

'Barbara, it's Arthur Dunbar.'

'Welcome back, Arthur. Did you have a nice time in Vancouver?'

'Couldn't have been better. In fact I'm considering moving out there when I retire.'

'We'll all miss you,' said Barbara. 'I'm not sure how the place will survive without you.'

'I'm sure it will,' said Arthur, 'but when are you expecting Mr Stratton back?'

'He and his wife flew to Miami on Friday. He'll be away for three weeks, so there couldn't be a better time for us to rob the bank.'

'And run away together,' laughed Arthur. 'Toronto's answer to Bonnie and Clyde! Still, while I'm the senior officer, could you keep me briefed if anything important arises?'

'Of course,' said Barbara. 'But as you well know, not a

lot happens in August while so many customers are away on holiday. But I'll give you a buzz if anything comes up.'

◄○►

Arthur checked his post every morning, but it wasn't until the sixth day that the first of the two letters landed on his desk. Arthur didn't rest on the seventh day, now he felt confident that Laidlaw was keeping his side of the bargain. He picked up the phone and pressed another button.

'Standing orders,' said a voice he recognized.

'Steve, it's Arthur Dunbar. I've just received a letter from Mr Macpherson, and he's instructed the bank to raise Mr and Mrs Laidlaw's monthly allowance.'

'I wish someone would do that for me,' said Steve.

'I'll send down a copy of the letter for your files,' said Arthur, ignoring the comment. 'And can you make sure that everything is in place for the September payment.'

'Of course, Mr Dunbar.'

The second letter took a little longer to arrive, and Arthur became quite anxious that the Laidlaws may have changed their mind, until the post boy delivered an envelope postmarked Ambrose on Monday morning, leaving him only five working days to complete the next part of his plan. But like a good Boy Scout, Arthur was well prepared.

He checked his watch. Buchan would still be at his desk for at least another couple of hours, but he needed to make an internal call before he contacted Edinburgh.

35

He picked up the phone, pressed another button and waited until the head of accounts came on the line.

'I'm sure you've seen a copy of the Macpherson letter,' he said.

'Yes I have,' replied Caldercroft, 'and I'm sorry, Arthur, because you must be disappointed after all these years.'

'It was bound to happen at some time,' said Arthur.

'Sad that it's just when you're leaving. Will you get in touch with Mr Macpherson and try to persuade him to change his mind?'

'Not much point. He hasn't done so for the past twenty years, so why would he now?'

'I'm sure you're right,' said Caldercroft. 'But shouldn't we wait until Stratton gets back, and see how he wants to play it?'

'I'm afraid the new banking laws don't allow us that luxury,' said Arthur. 'If a client requests to move his account, we must carry out their wishes within fourteen days, and as you can see, the letter is dated the eleventh.'

'Perhaps we should call Mr Stratton in Miami, and alert him of the situation?'

'You call him if you want to, Reg . . .'

'No, no,' said Caldercroft. 'You're in charge during the manager's absence, so what do you want me to do next?'

'Gather up all Mr Macpherson's bonds, stocks and any other financial instruments, and courier them to a Mr Buchan at RBS in Edinburgh, who appears to be the person he's appointed to take over the account. I'm just about to phone Buchan and find out when it will be convenient to complete the transfer. I'll keep you briefed.' He put the phone down.

Arthur took a deep breath and checked over his script one more time before he picked up the phone again and asked the switchboard operator to get him a number in Edinburgh. He waited to be put through.

'Good morning, Mr Buchan, my name is Arthur Dunbar, and I'm the senior VP at the National Bank of Toronto.'

'Good morning, Mr Dunbar,' said his opposite number. 'I've been expecting your call. I had a visit from a Mr Macpherson a couple of weeks ago, and he said you'd be in touch.'

'Indeed,' said Arthur, 'although we will be very sorry to be losing Mr Macpherson, a most valued client, but pleased he'll be moving to our partner bank in Edinburgh. And to that end,' said Arthur, trying to sound pompous, 'I have already given instructions to send all the necessary paperwork to you by courier, which I anticipate should be dealt with by the end of the week.'

'Thank you, said Buchan, 'and when will it be convenient for you to transfer Mr Macpherson's current account?'

'Would Thursday morning suit you? Around this time.'

'That should be fine. I'll make sure everything is in place to receive the funds on Thursday afternoon, and may I ask roughly how much we should be looking out for?'

'I can't be certain of the exact figure,' said Arthur, 'because I won't know the dollar–sterling exchange rate until that morning. But it will certainly be in excess of four million pounds.'

There was no response, and Arthur even wondered if they'd been cut off. 'Are you still there, Mr Buchan?'

'Yes, I am, Mr Dunbar,' Buchan eventually managed. 'And I look forward to hearing from you again on Thursday.'

—◇—

Mr Stratton returned from his holiday the following Monday, and had only been in his office for a few minutes before he called for the senior vice president.

'Why didn't you try and contact me in Miami?' were his first words as Arthur entered the room.

'As you can see,' said Arthur, placing his own typewritten letter on the desk, 'Mr Macpherson's instructions couldn't have been clearer, and as I have no way of contacting him other than by post, there wasn't a lot I could do.'

'You could have held things up, even flown to Scotland to see if you could get him to change his mind.'

'That would have been pointless,' said Arthur, 'as he had already visited RBS in Edinburgh and instructed a Mr Buchan to carry out the transfer as expeditiously as possible.'

'Which I see you did last Thursday.'

'Yes,' said Arthur. 'We just managed to complete the transaction within the time stipulated by the new government regulations.' Stratton pursed his lips. 'But a little coup I thought you would approve of,' continued Arthur, enjoying himself, 'the Toronto end handled the exchange from dollars into pounds sterling, earning the bank some 73,141 dollars.'

'A small compensation,' said Stratton begrudgingly.

'How kind of you to say so, Gerald.'

—◦—

Arthur spent his last month making sure everything was in apple pie order, no more than his mother would have expected, so by the time Reg Caldercroft moved into his office and took over as the new senior vice president, Arthur had only one responsibility left: preparing a farewell speech for his retirement party.

'I think I can safely say,' said Mr Stratton, 'that few people have served this bank more conscientiously, and certainly none longer, than Arthur Dunbar. Twenty-nine years, in fact.'

'Twenty-nine years and seven months,' said Arthur with some feeling, and several of the longer-serving staff stifled a laugh.

'We're all going to miss you, Arthur.' The insincere smile returning to the manager's lips. 'And we wish you a long and happy retirement when you leave us to join your family in Vancouver.'

Loud 'hear, hears' followed this statement.

'And on behalf of the bank,' continued Stratton, 'it's my pleasure to present you with a Rolex Oyster watch, and I hope whenever you look at it, you will be reminded of your time at the bank. Let's all raise a glass to our senior vice president, Arthur Dunbar.'

'To Arthur,' said over a hundred voices, as they raised their glasses in the air, which was quickly followed by cries of 'speech, speech!' from the guests. They all fell silent when Arthur walked up to the front and took Stratton's place.

'I'd like to begin,' said Arthur, 'by thanking those people, and in particular Barbara, for organizing such a splendid party, and to all of you for this magnificent gift. And to you, Gerald,' he said, turning to face the manager, 'I must say it will be quite hard to forget who gave me the watch, when engraved on the back is the inscription, "To Arthur, from all his colleagues at NBT".' Everyone laughed and applauded as Arthur strapped the watch on his wrist. 'And if any of you should ever find yourself at a loose end in Vancouver, do please look me up.' He didn't add, but should you do so, you won't find me.

Arthur was touched by how warm the applause was when he rejoined the guests.

'We'll all miss you,' said Barbara.

Arthur smiled at the biggest gem in the bank. 'And I'll miss you,' he admitted.

4

ARTHUR LEFT the bank at six o'clock on quarter day. He took the bus back to his small apartment and packed up all his belongings before spending his last night in Toronto.

The following morning, after handing over the keys to his apartment to the janitor, he took a cab to the airport. He only made one stop on the journey, when he donated four packed suitcases of his past to a grateful volunteer worker at the local Red Cross shop.

After checking in at the domestic terminal, Arthur boarded the midday flight for Vancouver. On arrival on the west coast, he collected his only suitcase from the carousel, and took a shuttle bus across to the international terminal. He waited in line before purchasing a business-class ticket to London, which he paid for with the last of his Canadian dollars. By the time Arthur boarded the plane he was so exhausted he slept for almost the entire flight.

When he landed at Heathrow and had passed through Customs, he once again transferred to terminal five and purchased a ticket to Edinburgh, also with cash. Arthur checked the departure board, and although he had an hour to spare, he made his way slowly across to gate 43. He stopped at every lavatory en route, locked himself into a cubicle, ripped out one page of his Canadian passport, tore it into little pieces and flushed it down the toilet.

By the time Arthur reached the check-in desk, all he had left of his old passport was the cover. Mr Dunbar dropped it into the bottom of a waste bin outside McDonald's.

'Will all passengers . . .'

Mr Macpherson stepped onto the plane.

On arrival in Edinburgh, Arthur took a taxi to the Caledonian Hotel and checked in.

'Welcome back,' said the desk clerk, as he checked his credit card against the customer's reservation. He handed him a room key and said, 'You've been upgraded, Mr Macpherson.'

'Thank you,' said Arthur, who was shown up to a small suite on the sixth floor, to be greeted with a bottle of champagne in an ice bucket, and a handwritten note of welcome from the manager. He gave the bellboy a handsome tip.

Once he'd unpacked, he called Mr Buchan and made an appointment to see him later that afternoon. Following a light lunch in the brasserie, Arthur took a stroll along Princes Street and arrived outside the bank with a few minutes to spare.

'How nice to see you again, Mr Macpherson,' said

Buchan, leaping up from behind his desk when Arthur entered the account manager's office.

'It's nice to see you too,' said Arthur, as the two men shook hands.

'Can I offer you a tea or coffee?' asked Buchan once his client was seated.

'No, thank you. I only wanted to check that my bank in Toronto had carried out the transfer, and there hadn't been any problems.'

'None that I'm aware of,' said Buchan. 'In fact, the transfer couldn't have gone more smoothly, thanks to Mr Dunbar, and I'm looking forward to representing you in the future. So can I ask, Mr Macpherson, is there anything you require at the moment?'

'A new credit card and some chequebooks.'

'Can I suggest our gold club card,' said Buchan, 'which has a daily credit limit of one thousand pounds, with no security checks, and I've already put in an order for some new chequebooks, which should be with us by Monday. Would you like me to forward them on to Ambrose Hall?'

'That won't be necessary,' said Arthur, 'as I intend to spend a few days in Edinburgh before I return to Ambrose. So perhaps I can drop in on Monday and pick them up.'

'Then I'll put a foot on the pedal and make sure they're ready for you to collect by then.'

'And my old NBT card?' asked Arthur.

'We'll cancel that when we hand over the new one on

Monday. Do you have enough cash to see you through the weekend?'

'More than enough,' said Arthur.

—◄o►—

Arthur left the bank and began walking back down Princes Street. What he hadn't told Buchan was that he intended to do some shopping before he headed for Ambrose, and even take in a concert or recital. In fact he dropped into four shops on his way back to the hotel, and purchased three suits, six silk shirts, two pairs of Church's shoes and an overcoat in the sale. Arthur had done more shopping in three hours than he'd previously managed in three years. As he continued down Princes Street, Arthur stopped to look at the painting in the window of Munro's, a Peploe that he much admired. But he already had half a dozen of his own. In any case, he decided it might not be wise to enter the gallery where Mr Macpherson had purchased so many pictures in the past, so he continued on his way back to the hotel.

After a cold shower and a change of clothes, Arthur made his way down to the hotel dining room, where he enjoyed an Aberdeen Angus steak with all the trimmings, and a bottle of red wine he had read about in one of the colour supplements.

By the time he'd signed the bill – he nearly forgot his name – he was ready for a good night's sleep. He was passing Scott's Bar on his way to the lifts when he turned and saw her image in the mirror. She was sitting on a stool at the far end of the bar sipping a glass of champagne. Arthur continued on towards the lifts, and when one opened, he hesitated, turned around and began walking slowly back towards the bar. Could she really have been that attractive? There was only one way he was going to find out. In any case, someone had probably joined her by now.

A second look, and he was even more captivated. She must have been about forty, and the elegant green dress that rested just above her knees only convinced Arthur she couldn't possibly be alone. He strolled up to the bar and took a seat on a stool two places away from her. He ordered a drink, but he didn't have the nerve to even glance in her direction, and certainly wouldn't have considered striking up a conversation.

'Are you here for the conference?' she asked.

Arthur swung round and stared into those green eyes before murmuring, 'What conference?'

'The garden centres annual conference.'

'No,' said Arthur. 'I'm on holiday. But is that why you're here?'

'Yes, I run a small garden centre in Durham. Are you a gardener by any chance?'

Arthur thought about his flat in Toronto where he'd had a window box, and Ambrose Hall, that couldn't have been less than a thousand acres.

'No,' he managed. 'Always lived in a city,' he added, as she drained her champagne. 'Can I get you another?'

'Thank you,' she said, allowing the barman to refill her glass. 'My name's Marianne.'

'I'm Sandy,' he said.

'And what do you do, Sandy?'

'I dabble in stocks and shares,' he replied, taking on the persona of Macpherson. 'And when you said "run", does that mean you're the boss?'

'I wish,' she said, and by the time Marianne's glass had been refilled three times, he'd discovered she was divorced, her husband had run away with a woman half his age, no children, and she had planned to go to the Schubert concert at the Usher Hall that night only to find it was sold out. After another drink, he even found out she didn't consider Brahms to be in the same class as Beethoven. He was already wondering how far the journey was from Edinburgh to Durham.

'Would you like another drink?' he asked.

'No, thank you,' she replied. 'I ought to be getting to bed if I'm still hoping to make the opening session tomorrow.'

'Why don't we go up to my suite? I have a bottle of champagne, and no one to share it with.' Arthur couldn't believe what he'd just said, and assumed she'd get up and leave without another word, and might even slap his face. He was just about to apologize, when Marianne said, 'That sounds fun.' She slipped off her stool, took his hand and said, 'Which floor are you on, Sandy?'

In the past, Arthur had only dreamed of such a night, or

read about it in novels by Harold Robbins. After they'd made love a third time, she said, 'I ought to be getting back to my room, Sandy, if I'm not going to fall asleep during the president's address.'

'When does the conference end?' asked Arthur, as he sat up and watched her getting dressed.

'Usually around four.'

'Why don't I try to get a couple of tickets for the Schubert concert, and then we could have dinner afterwards.'

'What a lovely idea,' said Marianne. 'Shall we meet in reception at seven tomorrow evening?' She giggled. 'This evening,' she added, as she bent down and kissed him.

'See you then,' he said, and by the time the door had closed, Arthur had fallen into a deep contented sleep.

―◦―

When Arthur woke the following morning, he couldn't stop thinking about Marianne, and decided to buy her a present and give it to her at dinner that evening. But first he must get two tickets, the best in the house for a show that was obviously sold out, and then ask the desk clerk which he considered was the finest restaurant in Edinburgh.

Arthur had a long shower, and found himself humming the aria from Mendelssohn's Midsummer Night's Dream. He continued to hum as he put on a new shirt, new suit and began to think about what sort of present Marianne would like. Mustn't be over the top, but shouldn't leave her in any doubt he considered last night so much more than a one-night stand.

He went to his bedside table to pick up his wallet and watch, but they weren't there. He opened the drawer, and stared at a copy of Gideon's Bible. He quickly checked the table on the other side of the bed, and then the bathroom, and finally his new suit that was strewn on the floor. He sat on the end of the bed for some time, unwilling to accept the truth. He didn't want to believe such a divine creature could be a common thief.

He reluctantly picked up the phone by the side of the bed and dialled Mr Buchan's private number at the Royal Bank of Scotland. He sat there in a daze until he heard a voice he recognized on the other end of the line.

'I'm sorry to bother you,' said Arthur, 'but I've lost my credit card.'

'That's not a problem,' said Buchan. 'Happens all the time. I'll cancel it immediately and your new one will be ready for collection on Monday morning. If you need some cash in the meantime, just pop in and I'll arrange it.'

'No, I've got enough to get me through until Monday,' said Arthur, not wanting to admit that his money had also been stolen.

Arthur went downstairs for breakfast, and wasn't surprised to discover that there was no garden centres conference, and no one called Marianne registered at the hotel. When he left the Caledonian to go for a walk after breakfast, it was back to window shopping and he even spotted the ideal present for Marianne. It didn't help. And when he passed Usher Hall on the way back, there was a queue for returns. At least that was true.

It was a long weekend of walks, hotel food and watching B movies in his room that he'd already seen. When he walked past Scott's Bar on Saturday night and saw an attractive young blonde sitting alone, he just kept on walking. By Monday he'd exhausted the hotel menu and the films of the week and just wanted to get back to Ambrose Hall and begin his new life. The only surprise was that he still couldn't get Marianne out of his mind.

5

By the time Arthur had packed his bags on Monday morning, he'd decided the loss of a couple of hundred pounds and a watch he'd never cared for, was a fair exchange for the best night he'd ever had in his life.

He checked his watch. It wasn't there. Arthur smiled for the first time in days. Once he'd seen Buchan, he would take the first train to Ambrose and try to forget the whole incident, but he knew he wouldn't be able to. He was feeling a little better by the time he left the hotel to keep his appointment with Mr Buchan, and when he walked into the bank, his secretary was standing in the hall waiting to greet him. A gesture, he realized, that was extended to only the most important customers.

'I hope you had an enjoyable weekend, Mr Macpherson?' she said, as she accompanied Arthur through to Mr Buchan's office.

'Yes, thank you,' he replied politely, as she opened the door and stepped aside to allow him to enter.

Arthur froze on the spot when he saw Mr Stratton

seated to the right of Mr Buchan, with a large burly man he didn't recognize seated on his left.

'Sit down, Dunbar,' said Stratton, as the door closed behind him.

Arthur obeyed the order as if they were back in Toronto, but said nothing.

'It wasn't difficult for me to work out what you've been up to for the past year,' said Stratton, 'and at least we caught up with you before you could do any real damage. We have Chief Inspector Mullins of the Edinburgh city police,' he added, revealing who the third person was, 'to thank for that.'

Arthur still didn't speak, although he would have liked to ask the policeman how long his sentence was likely to be, but satisfied himself with, 'How did you find out?'

'The watch,' said Chief Inspector Mullins matter-of-factly. '"To Arthur, from all his colleagues at NBT". Once we'd cracked NBT, the rest was easy. And after she'd described you as a nice gentleman with a mid-Atlantic accent, one call to the bank and Mr Stratton even told us he'd presented you with the Rolex Oyster.'

'And Marianne, how did you catch her?'

'She tried to buy a train ticket to Durham with your credit card, but fortunately Mr Buchan had already cancelled it.'

'And as far as I can tell,' said Stratton, taking over, 'you've only spent 2,782 dollars of Mr Macpherson's money. However, that doesn't include the 73,141 dollars the bank will have to return to Mr Macpherson's private account, following the abortive exchange rate deal.'

'And a further 49,124 pounds,' said Buchan, 'that will have to be charged to NBT after converting the four million back into dollars.'

'Mr Buchan has already supplied me with all the share certificates, bonds and other financial instruments which I will be taking back to Toronto later today, and once I return, Mr Macpherson's account will be repaid in full. So with a bit of luck, he will never find out what happened. However,' Stratton continued, 'you have cost the NBT 123,468 dollars, not to mention the irreparable damage you might have caused to the National Bank of Toronto's reputation had this story ever got out. But, thanks to the cooperation of the Edinburgh police, to whom we will be eternally grateful,' continued Stratton, nodding in the chief inspector's direction, 'if you will agree to cover any costs, they will not press charges.'

'And if I don't?' said Arthur.

'As a senior banking officer, in a position of trust,' said Chief Inspector Mullins, 'you could be looking at six to eight years in a Scottish prison. I would'nae recommend it, laddie,' he paused, 'given the choice.'

Mr Stratton stood up and walked down from the other end of the table and handed over a cheque made out to the bank for $123,468. All it needed was a signature.

'But that would almost clean me out.'

'Perhaps you should have thought about that in the first place,' said Stratton, handing him a pen.

Arthur reluctantly signed the cheque, accepting that the alternative, as Mullins had so subtly pointed out, wasn't that attractive.

Stratton retrieved the cheque and placed it in his wallet. He then turned to the chief inspector and said, 'Like you, we will not be pressing charges.'

Mullins looked disappointed.

Typical Stratton, thought Arthur. Make sure you cover your own backside, and to hell with everyone else. Arthur even wondered if the board would ever be told what had really happened. But Stratton hadn't finished. He picked up a carrier bag from under his chair, and emptied a pile of Canadian dollars onto the table in front of Arthur.

'Your account has been closed,' he said, 'and the bank is no longer willing to do business with you in the future.'

Arthur slowly gathered up the neat cellophane packages, aware that he would even be paying for Stratton's first-class flight back to Toronto. He dropped the money into the carrier bag.

'And what about my watch, chief inspector?' said Arthur, turning to face Mullins.

'Mrs Dawson comes up in front of the magistrate at ten o'clock tomorrow morning, so you can collect it any time after that, but not until she's been sentenced.' He smiled at Arthur for the first time.

'I don't suppose you'd be willing to appear as a witness for the Crown?' he said, raising an eyebrow.

Arthur smiled back. 'You suppose correctly, chief inspector. I wouldn't, even if you'd made it a condition.'

Mullins frowned as Arthur rose from his place, and quietly left the room; no smiles, no handshakes, and certainly no one accompanied him to the front door. He left the bank in a daze and began to make his way slowly back to the hotel, not certain what to do next.

He'd only gone about a hundred yards along Princes Street, when he spotted a sign on a window in neat black letters, Henderson & Henderson, Attorneys at Law.

6

WHEN THE DEFENDANT took her place in the dock, she looked tired and vulnerable.

A court officer rose and read out the charges. 'Marianne Dawson, you come before the court on three charges. One: that you stole a credit card from a Mr Macpherson, and attempted to use it to purchase a rail ticket to Durham. How do you plead to this charge, guilty or not guilty?'

'Guilty,' said the defendant, almost in a whisper.

'The second charge,' continued the officer, 'is that you did steal a sum of around two hundred pounds from the said Mr Macpherson. How do you plead, guilty or not guilty?'

'Guilty,' she repeated.

'And the third count is that you did steal a Rolex Oyster watch also from the same gentleman. How do you plead, guilty or not guilty?'

Marianne looked up and facing the magistrate said quietly, 'Guilty.'

The chairman of the magistrates stared down into the well of the court and asked, 'Is the defendant represented?'

A tall distinguished-looking man, dressed in a pin-striped suit, white shirt and black tie, rose from the bench and said, 'I have the privilege of representing Mrs Dawson.'

The Justice of the Peace was surprised to find one of Edinburgh's leading advocates appearing before him on such a minor case.

'Mr Henderson, as your client has pleaded guilty to all three charges, I presume you will be offering a plea in mitigation?'

'I most certainly will, sir,' he said, tugging the lapels of his jacket. 'I would like to start by bringing to the attention of the court that Mrs Dawson has recently experienced a most acrimonious divorce, and despite the family division awarding her alimony, her husband has made no attempt to fulfil his responsibility, even after a court order was issued against him. Until recently,' continued Mr Henderson, 'Mrs Dawson held a senior management position at the Durham Garden Centre, until it was taken over by Scotsdales, and she was made redundant. I feel sure the Bench will also take into consideration that this is a first offence, other than a parking fine four years ago. However, Mrs Dawson is not only extremely remorseful, but determined to pay Mr Macpherson back every penny she owes him, just as soon as she can find a job. I would finally like to point out that until today, Mrs Dawson enjoyed an unblemished reputation as an upright citizen, which I hope the Bench will take into consideration before passing sentence.'

'I am grateful to you, Mr Henderson,' said the justice. 'Please allow me a few moments to consult my colleagues.'

Henderson bowed, as the chairman and his two colleagues discussed the case among themselves, before coming to an agreement.

The chairman turned back to face the defendant.

'Mrs Dawson,' he began, 'despite learned counsel's moving plea in mitigation, someone in your position must have been well aware they were breaking the law.' Marianne bowed her head. 'So I am left with no choice but to sentence you to six months in prison, which will be suspended for two years. However, should you appear before me again, I will not hesitate to issue you with a custodial sentence. But on this occasion, I shall order you to pay a fine of two hundred pounds.' He switched his attention back to Mr Henderson, and asked, 'Is the defendant able to pay this sum?'

Mr Henderson turned round and looked towards the back of the courtroom where his client was seated. Arthur nodded.

◄○►

Arthur took a piece of headed paper from the letter rack on his desk and placed it in the typewriter.

Dear Mr Stratton,
Thank you for your most recent letter, and the three new chequebooks that arrived this morning.

May I begin by placing on record how much I appreciate the years of dedicated service Mr Arthur Dunbar carried out on my behalf, and would you be kind enough to pass on my best wishes to him and the hope he will have a long and happy retirement.

I have checked my latest accounts which appear to be in order. However, I will be writing to you at the end of the quarter concerning some future investments I am presently considering.

I should also like you to know that I have recently married, so you may find a new pattern will emerge in some of my transactions. My wife and I intend to travel abroad occasionally, to visit the great concert halls and opera houses of Europe. While we're away, Mr and Mrs Laidlaw will continue to run Ambrose Hall, so you can expect the usual bills for household expenses in addition to their monthly salaries.

May I also add . . .

There was a knock at the door, and Arthur stopped typing. 'Come in.'

Morag popped her head round the door and said, 'I just wondered what you and Mrs Macpherson would like for lunch? I still have some of that game pie you're rather partial to.'

'Perfect,' said Arthur, 'but not too much. Mrs Macpherson has already chastised me for putting on weight.'

'And Mrs Macpherson also asked me to remind you

that you're going into Edinburgh this evening for some concert.'

'Not some concert, Morag, Beethoven's Third at the Usher Hall.'

'Will there be anything else, sir?'

'Yes, I'm just finishing off a letter to Mr Stratton, so could you ask Hamish to come up. I'd like him to drive into the village and post it.'

'Of course, sir.'

Arthur returned to the letter.

> *May I also add how delighted I was to learn that you will personally be supervising my account in the future. It gives me succour to know that my affairs will be in such safe hands.*
>
> *Yours sincerely*

There was a knock on the door and Mr Laidlaw walked in.

'You asked to see me, sir?'

'Yes, Hamish. Just a signature.'

Turn the page to read an extract from

ONLY TIME WILL TELL

the captivating first instalment in the
number one bestselling series phenomenon,
The Clifton Chronicles.

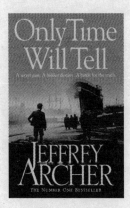

PRELUDE: MAISIE CLIFTON
1919

THIS STORY WOULD never have been written if I hadn't become pregnant. Mind you, I had always planned to lose my virginity on the works outing to Weston-super-Mare, just not to that particular man.

Arthur Clifton was born in Still House Lane, just like me; even went to the same school, Merrywood Elementary, but as I was two years younger than him he didn't know I existed. All the girls in my class had a crush on him, and not just because he captained the school football team.

Although Arthur had never shown any interest in me while I was at school, that changed soon after he'd returned from the Western Front. I'm not even sure he realized who I was when he asked me for a dance that Saturday night at the Palais but, to be fair, I had to look twice before I recognized him because he'd grown a pencil moustache and had his hair slicked back like Ronald Colman. He didn't look at another girl that night, and after we'd danced the last waltz I knew it would only be a matter of time before he asked me to marry him.

Arthur held my hand as we walked back home, and when we reached my front door he tried to kiss me. I turned away. After all, the Reverend Watts had told me often enough that I had to stay pure until the day I was married, and Miss Monday, our choir mistress, warned me that men only wanted one thing, and once they'd got it, they quickly lost interest. I often wondered if Miss Monday spoke from experience.

The following Saturday, Arthur invited me to the flicks to see Lillian Gish in *Broken Blossoms*, and although I allowed him to put an arm around my shoulder, I still didn't let him kiss me. He didn't make a fuss. Truth is, Arthur was rather shy.

The next Saturday I did allow him to kiss me, but when he tried to put a hand inside my blouse, I pushed him away. In fact I didn't let him do that until he'd proposed, bought a ring and the Reverend Watts had read the banns a second time.

My brother Stan told me that I was the last known virgin on our side of the River Avon, though I suspect most of his conquests were in his mind. Still, I decided the time had come, and when better than the works outing to Weston-super-Mare with the man I was going to marry in a few weeks' time?

However, as soon as Arthur and Stan got off the chara-banc, they headed straight for the nearest pub. But I'd spent the past month planning for this moment, so when I got off the coach, like a good girl guide, I was prepared.

I was walking towards the pier feeling pretty fed up when I became aware someone was following me. I looked around and was surprised when I saw who it was. He caught up with me and asked if I was on my own.

'Yes,' I said, aware that by now Arthur would be on his third pint.

When he put a hand on my bum, I should have slapped his face, but for several reasons I didn't. To start with, I thought about the advantages of having sex with someone I wasn't likely to come across again. And I have to admit I was flattered by his advances.

By the time Arthur and Stan would have been downing their eighth pints, he'd booked us into a guest house just off the seafront. They seemed to have a special rate for visitors who had no plans to spend the night. He started kissing me even before we'd reached the first landing, and once the bedroom door was closed he quickly undid the buttons of my blouse. It obviously wasn't his first time. In fact, I'm pretty sure I wasn't the first girl he'd had on a works outing. Otherwise, how did he know about the special rates?

I must confess I hadn't expected it to be all over quite so quickly. Once he'd climbed off me, I disappeared into the bathroom, while he sat on the end of the bed and lit up a fag. Perhaps it would be better the second time, I thought. But when I came back out, he was nowhere to be seen. I have to admit I was disappointed.

I might have felt more guilty about being unfaithful to

Arthur if he hadn't been sick all over me on the journey back to Bristol.

The next day I told my mum what had happened, without letting on who the bloke was. After all, she hadn't met him, and was never likely to. Mum told me to keep my mouth shut as she didn't want to have to cancel the wedding, and even if I did turn out to be pregnant, no one would be any the wiser, as Arthur and I would be married by the time anyone noticed.

HARRY CLIFTON
1920–1933

1

I WAS TOLD my father was killed in the war.

Whenever I questioned my mother about his death, she didn't say any more than that he'd served with the Royal Gloucestershire Regiment and had been killed fighting on the Western Front only days before the Armistice was signed. Grandma said my dad had been a brave man, and once when we were alone in the house she showed me his medals. My grandpa rarely offered an opinion on anything, but then he was deaf as a post so he might not have heard the question in the first place.

The only other man I can remember was my uncle Stan, who used to sit at the top of the table at breakfast time. When he left of a morning I would often follow him to the city docks, where he worked. Every day I spent at the dockyard was an adventure. Cargo ships coming from distant lands and unloading their wares: rice, sugar, bananas, jute and many other things I'd never heard of.

Once the holds had been emptied, the dockers would load them with salt, apples, tin, even coal (my least favourite, because it was an obvious clue to what I'd been doing all day and annoyed my mother), before they set off again to I knew not where. I always wanted to help my uncle Stan unload whatever ship had docked that morning, but he just laughed, saying, 'All in good time, my lad.' It couldn't be soon enough for me, but, without any warning, school got in the way.

I was sent to Merrywood Elementary when I was six and I thought it was a complete waste of time. What was the point of school when I could learn all I needed to at the docks? I wouldn't have bothered to go back the following day if my mother hadn't dragged me to the front gates, deposited me and returned at four o'clock that afternoon to take me home.

I didn't realize Mum had other plans for my future, which didn't include joining Uncle Stan in the shipyard.

Once Mum had dropped me off each morning, I would hang around in the yard until she was out of sight, then slope off to the docks. I made sure I was always back at the school gates when she returned to pick me up in the afternoon. On the way home, I would tell her everything I'd done at school that day. I was good at making up stories, but it wasn't long before she discovered that was all they were: stories.

One or two other boys from my school also used to hang around the docks, but I kept my distance from them.

They were older and bigger, and used to thump me if I got in their way. I also had to keep an eye out for Mr Haskins, the chief ganger, because if he ever found me loitering, to use his favourite word, he would send me off with a kick up the backside and the threat: 'If I see you loiterin' round here again, my lad, I'll report you to the headmaster.'

Occasionally Haskins decided he'd seen me once too often and I'd be reported to the headmaster, who would leather me before sending me back to my classroom. My form master, Mr Holcombe, never let on if I didn't show up for his class, but then he was a bit soft. Whenever my mum found out I'd been playing truant, she couldn't hide her anger and would stop my halfpenny-a-week pocket money. But despite the occasional punch from an older boy, regular leatherings from the headmaster and the loss of my pocket money, I still couldn't resist the draw of the docks.

I made only one real friend while I 'loitered' around the dockyard. His name was Old Jack Tar. Mr Tar lived in an abandoned railway carriage at the end of the sheds. Uncle Stan told me to keep away from Old Jack because he was a stupid, dirty old tramp. He didn't look that dirty to me, certainly not as dirty as Stan, and it wasn't long before I discovered he wasn't stupid either.

After lunch with my uncle Stan, one bite of his Marmite sandwich, his discarded apple core and a swig of beer, I would be back at school in time for a game of football; the only activity I considered it worth turning up for. After all, when I left school I was going to captain Bristol City, or build a ship that would sail around the world. If Mr Holcombe kept his mouth shut and the ganger didn't report me to the headmaster, I could go for days without being found out, and as long as I avoided the coal barges and was standing by the school gate at four o'clock every afternoon, my mother would never be any the wiser.

◄◦►

Every other Saturday, Uncle Stan would take me to watch Bristol City at Ashton Gate. On Sunday mornings, Mum used to cart me off to Holy Nativity Church, something I couldn't find a way of getting out of. Once the Reverend Watts had given the final blessing, I would run all the way to the recreation ground and join my mates for a game of football before returning home in time for dinner.

By the time I was seven it was clear to anyone who knew anything about the game of football that I was never going to get into the school team, let alone captain Bristol City. But that was when I discovered that God had given me one small gift, and it wasn't in my feet.

To begin with, I didn't notice that anyone who sat near me in church on a Sunday morning stopped singing whenever I opened my mouth. I wouldn't have given it a second thought if Mum hadn't suggested I join the choir. I laughed scornfully; after all, everyone knew the choir was only for girls and cissies. I would have dismissed the idea out of hand if the Reverend Watts hadn't told me that choirboys were paid a penny for funerals and tuppence for weddings; my first experience of bribery. But even after I'd reluctantly agreed to take a vocal test, the devil decided to place an obstacle in my path, in the form of Miss Eleanor E. Monday.

I would never have come across Miss Monday if she hadn't been the choir mistress at Holy Nativity. Although she was only five feet three, and looked as though a gust of wind might blow her away, no one tried to take the mickey. I have a feeling that even the devil would have been frightened of Miss Monday, because the Reverend Watts certainly was.

I agreed to take a vocal test, but not before my mum had handed over a month's pocket money in advance. The following Sunday I stood in line with a group of other lads and waited to be called.

'You will always be on time for choir practice,' Miss Monday announced, fixing a gimlet eye on me. I stared back defiantly. 'You will never speak, unless spoken to.' I somehow managed to remain silent. 'And during the service, you will concentrate at all times.' I reluctantly nodded. And then, God bless her, she gave me a way out. 'But most importantly,' she declared, placing her hands on her hips, 'within twelve weeks, you will be expected to pass a reading and writing test, so that I can be sure you are able to tackle a new anthem or an unfamiliar psalm.'

I was pleased to have fallen at the first hurdle. But as

I was to discover, Miss Eleanor E. Monday didn't give up easily.

'What piece have you chosen to sing, child?' she asked me when I reached the front of the line.

'I haven't chosen anything,' I told her.

She opened a hymn book, handed it to me and sat down at the piano. I smiled at the thought that I might still be able to make the second half of our Sunday morning football game. She began to play a familiar tune, and when I saw my mother glaring at me from the front row of pews, I decided I'd better go through with it, just to keep her happy.

'*All things bright and beautiful, all creatures great and small. All things wise and wonderful . . .*' A smile had appeared on Miss Monday's face long before I reached '*the Lord God made them all*'.

'What's your name, child?' she asked.

'Harry Clifton, miss.'

'Harry Clifton, you will report for choir practice on Mondays, Wednesdays and Fridays at six o'clock sharp.' Turning to the boy standing behind me, she said, 'Next!'

I promised my mum I'd be on time for the first choir practice, even though I knew it would be my last, as Miss Monday would soon realize I couldn't read or write. And it would have been my last, if it hadn't been obvious to anyone listening that my singing voice was in a different class to that of any other boy in the choir. In fact, the moment I opened my mouth, everyone fell silent, and the looks of admiration, even awe, that I had desperately sought on the football field, were happening in church. Miss Monday pretended not to notice.

After she dismissed us, I didn't go home, but ran all the way to the docks so I could ask Mr Tar what I should do about the fact that I couldn't read or write. I listened carefully to the old man's advice, and the next day I went back to school and took my place in Mr Holcombe's class. The schoolmaster couldn't hide his surprise when he saw me sitting in the front row, and was even more surprised when I paid close attention to the morning lesson for the first time.

Mr Holcombe began by teaching me the alphabet, and within days I could write out all twenty-six letters, if not always in the correct order. My mum would have helped me when I got home in the afternoon but, like the rest of my family, she also couldn't read or write.

Uncle Stan could just about scrawl his signature, and although he could tell the difference between a packet of Wills's Star and Wild Woodbines, I was fairly sure he couldn't actually read the labels. Despite his unhelpful mutterings, I set about writing the alphabet on any piece of scrap paper I could find. Uncle Stan didn't seem to notice that the torn-up newspaper in the privy was always covered in letters.

Once I'd mastered the alphabet, Mr Holcombe introduced me to a few simple words: 'dog', 'cat', 'mum' and 'dad'. That was when I first asked him about my dad, hoping that he might be able to tell me something about him. After all, he seemed to know everything. But he seemed puzzled that I knew so little about my own dad. A week later he wrote my first four-letter word on the blackboard, 'book', and then five, 'house', and six, 'school'. By the end of the month, I could write my first sentence, 'The quick brown fox jumps over the lazy dog', which, Mr Holcombe pointed out, contained every letter in the alphabet. I checked, and he turned out to be right.

By the end of term I could spell 'anthem', 'psalm' and even 'hymn', although Mr Holcombe kept reminding me I still dropped my aitches whenever I spoke. But then we broke up for the holidays and I began to worry I would never pass Miss Monday's demanding test without Mr Holcombe's help. And that might have been the case, if Old Jack hadn't taken his place.

◄◊►

I was half an hour early for choir practice on the Friday evening when I knew I would have to pass my second test if I hoped to continue as a member of the choir. I sat silently in the stalls, hoping Miss Monday would pick on someone else before she called on me.

I had already passed the first test with what Miss Monday had described as flying colours. We had all been asked to recite *The Lord's Prayer*. This was not a problem for me, because for as long as I could remember my mum knelt by my bed each night and repeated the familiar words before tucking me up. However, Miss Monday's next test was to prove far more demanding.

By this time, the end of our second month, we were expected to read a psalm out loud, in front of the rest of the choir. I chose Psalm 121, which I also knew off by heart, having sung it so often in the past. *I will lift up mine eyes unto the hills, from whence cometh my help.* I could only hope that my help cometh from the Lord. Although I was able to turn to the correct page in the psalm book, as I could now count from one to a hundred, I feared Miss Monday would realize that I was unable to follow every verse line by line. If she did, she didn't let on, because I remained in the choir stalls for another month while two other miscreants – her word, not that I knew what it meant until I asked Mr Holcombe the next day – were dispatched back to the congregation.

When the time came for me to take the third and final test, I was ready for it. Miss Monday asked those of us who remained to write out the Ten Commandments in the correct order without referring to the Book of Exodus.

The choir mistress turned a blind eye to the fact that I placed theft ahead of murder, couldn't spell 'adultery', and certainly didn't know what it meant. Only after two other miscreants were summarily dismissed for lesser offences did I realize just how exceptional my voice must be.

On the first Sunday of Advent, Miss Monday announced that she had selected three new trebles – or 'little angels', as the Reverend Watts was wont to describe us – to join her choir, the remainder having been rejected for committing such unforgivable sins as chattering during the sermon, sucking a gobstopper and, in the case of two boys, being caught playing conkers during the *Nunc Dimittis*.

The following Sunday, I dressed up in a long blue cassock with a ruffled white collar. I alone was allowed to wear a bronze medallion of the Virgin Mother around my neck, to show that I had been selected as the treble soloist. I would have proudly worn the medallion all the way back home, even to school the next morning, to show off to the rest of the lads, if only Miss Monday hadn't retrieved it at the end of each service.

On Sundays I was transported into another world, but I feared this state of delirium could not last for ever.

2

WHEN UNCLE STAN rose in the morning, he somehow managed to wake the entire household. No one complained, as he was the breadwinner in the family, and in any case he was cheaper and more reliable than an alarm clock.

The first noise Harry would hear was the bedroom door slamming. This would be followed by his uncle tramping along the creaky wooden landing, down the stairs and out of the house. Then another door would slam as he disappeared into the privy. If anyone was still asleep, the rush of water as Uncle Stan pulled the chain, followed by two more slammed doors before he returned to the bedroom, served to remind them that Stan expected his breakfast to be on the table by the time he walked into the kitchen. He only had a wash and a shave on Saturday evenings before going off to the Palais or the Odeon. He took a bath four times a year on quarter-day. No one was going to accuse Stan of wasting his hard-earned cash on soap.

Maisie, Harry's mum, would be next up, leaping out of bed moments after the first slammed door. There would be a bowl of porridge on the stove by the time Stan came out of the privy. Grandma followed shortly afterwards, and would join her daughter in the kitchen before Stan had taken his place at the head of the table. Harry had to be down within five minutes of the first slammed door if he hoped to get any breakfast. The last to arrive in the kitchen would be Grandpa, who was so deaf he often managed to sleep through Stan's early morning ritual. This daily routine in the Clifton household never varied. When you've only got one outside privy, one sink and one towel, order becomes a necessity.

By the time Harry was splashing his face with a trickle of cold water, his mother would be serving breakfast in the kitchen: two thickly sliced pieces of bread covered in lard for Stan, and four thin slices for the rest of the family, which she would toast if there was any coal left in the sack dumped outside the front door every Monday. Once Stan had finished his porridge, Harry would be allowed to lick the bowl.

A large brown pot of tea was always brewing on the hearth, which Grandma would pour into a variety of mugs through a silver-plated Victorian tea strainer she had inherited from her mother. While the other members of the family enjoyed a mug of unsweetened tea – sugar was only for high days and holidays – Stan would open his first bottle of beer, which he usually gulped down in one draught. He would then rise from the table and burp loudly before picking up his lunch box, which Grandma had prepared while he was having his breakfast: two Marmite sandwiches, a sausage, an apple, two more bottles of beer and a packet of five coffin nails. Once Stan had left for the docks, everyone began to talk at once.

Grandma always wanted to know who had visited the tea shop where her daughter worked as a waitress: what they ate, what they were wearing, where they sat; details of meals that were cooked on a stove in a room lit by electric light bulbs that didn't leave any candle wax, not to mention customers who sometimes left a thruppenny-bit tip, which Maisie had to split with the cook.

Maisie was more concerned to find out what Harry had done at school the previous day. She demanded a daily report, which didn't seem to interest Grandma, perhaps because she'd never been to school. Come to think of it, she'd never been to a tea shop either.

Grandpa rarely commented, because after four years

of loading and unloading an artillery field gun, morning, noon and night, he was so deaf he had to satisfy himself with watching their lips move and nodding from time to time. This could give outsiders the impression he was stupid, which the rest of the family knew to their cost he wasn't.

The family's morning routine only varied at weekends. On Saturdays, Harry would follow his uncle out of the kitchen, always remaining a pace behind him as he walked to the docks. On Sunday, Harry's mum would accompany the boy to Holy Nativity Church, where, from the third row of the pews, she would bask in the glory of the choir's treble soloist.

But today was Saturday. During the twenty-minute walk to the docks, Harry never opened his mouth unless his uncle spoke. Whenever he did, it invariably turned out to be the same conversation they'd had the previous Saturday.

'When are you goin' to leave school and do a day's work, young'un?' was always Uncle Stan's opening salvo.

'Not allowed to leave until I'm fourteen,' Harry reminded him. 'It's the law.'

'A bloody stupid law, if you ask me. I'd packed up school and was workin' on the docks by the time I were twelve,' Stan would announce as if Harry had never heard this profound observation before. Harry didn't bother to respond, as he already knew what his uncle's next sentence would be. 'And what's more I'd signed up to join Kitchener's army before my seventeenth birthday.'

'Tell me about the war, Uncle Stan,' said Harry, aware that this would keep him occupied for several hundred yards.

'Me and your dad joined the Royal Gloucestershire Regiment on the same day,' Stan said, touching his cloth cap as if saluting a distant memory. 'After twelve weeks' basic training at Taunton Barracks, we was shipped off to Wipers to fight the Boche. Once we got there, we spent most of our time cooped up in rat-infested trenches waiting to be told by some toffee-nosed officer that when the bugle sounded, we was going over the top, bayonets fixed, rifles firing as we advanced towards the enemy lines.' This would be followed by a long pause, after which Stan would add, 'I was one of the lucky ones. Got back to Blighty all ship-shape and Bristol fashion.' Harry could have predicted his next sentence word for word, but remained silent. 'You just don't know how lucky you are, my lad. I lost two brothers, your uncle Ray and your uncle Bert, and your father not only lost a brother, but his father, your other grandad, what you never met. A proper man, who could down a pint of beer faster than any docker I've ever come across.'

If Stan had looked down, he would have seen the boy mouthing his words, but today, to Harry's surprise, Uncle Stan added a sentence he'd never uttered before. 'And your dad would still be alive today, if only management had listened to me.'

Harry was suddenly alert. His dad's death had always been the subject of whispered conversations and hushed tones. But Uncle Stan clammed up, as if he realized he'd gone too far. Maybe next week, thought Harry, catching his uncle up and keeping in step with him as if they were two soldiers on a parade ground.

'So who are City playin' this afternoon?' asked Stan, back on script.

'Charlton Athletic,' Harry replied.

'They're a load of old cobblers.'

'They trounced us last season,' Harry reminded his uncle.

'Bloody lucky, if you ask me,' said Stan, and didn't open his mouth again. When they reached the entrance to the dockyard, Stan clocked in before heading off to the pen where he was working with a gang of other dockers, none of whom could afford to be a minute late. Unemployment was at an all-time high and too many young men were standing outside the gates waiting to take their place.

Harry didn't follow his uncle, because he knew that if Mr Haskins caught him hanging around the sheds he would get a clip round the ear, followed by a boot up the backside from his uncle for annoying the ganger. Instead, he set off in the opposite direction.

Harry's first port of call every Saturday morning was Old Jack Tar, who lived in the railway carriage at the other end of the dockyard. He had never told Stan about his regular visits because his uncle had warned him to avoid the old man at all costs.

'Probably hasn't had a bath in years,' said a man who washed once a quarter, and then only after Harry's mother complained about the smell.

But curiosity had long ago got the better of Harry, and one morning he'd crept up to the railway carriage on his hands and knees, lifted himself up and peeped through a window. The old man was sitting in first class, reading a book.

Old Jack turned to face him and said, 'Come on in, lad.' Harry jumped down, and didn't stop running until he reached his front door.

The following Saturday, Harry once again crawled up to the carriage and peered inside. Old Jack seemed to be fast asleep, but then Harry heard him say, 'Why don't you come in, my boy? I'm not going to bite you.'

Harry turned the heavy brass handle and tentatively pulled open the carriage door, but he didn't step inside. He just stared at the man seated in the centre of the carriage. It was hard to tell how old he was because his face was covered in a well-groomed salt-and-pepper beard, which made him look like the sailor on the Players Please packet. But he looked at Harry with a warmth in his eyes that Uncle Stan had never managed.

'Are you Old Jack Tar?' Harry ventured.

'That's what they call me,' the old man replied.

'And is this where you live?' Harry asked, glancing around the carriage, his eyes settling on a stack of old newspapers piled high on the opposite seat.

'Yes,' he replied. 'It's been my home for these past twenty years. Why don't you close the door and take a seat, young man?'

Harry gave the offer some thought before he jumped back out of the carriage and once again ran away.

The following Saturday, Harry did close the door, but he kept hold of the handle, ready to bolt if the old man as much as twitched a muscle. They stared at each other for some time before Old Jack asked, 'What's your name?'

'Harry.'

'And where do you go to school?'

'I don't go to school.'

'Then what are you hoping to do with your life, young man?'

'Join my uncle on the docks, of course,' Harry replied.

'Why would you want to do that?' said the old man.

'Why not?' Harry bristled. 'Don't you think I'm good enough?'

'You're far too good,' replied Old Jack. 'When I was your age,' he continued, 'I wanted to join the army, and nothing my old man could say or do would dissuade me.' For the next hour Harry stood, mesmerized, while Old Jack Tar reminisced about the docks, the city of Bristol, and lands beyond the sea that he couldn't have been taught about in geography lessons.

The following Saturday, and for more Saturdays than he would remember, Harry continued to visit Old Jack Tar. But he never once told his uncle or his mother, for fear they would stop him going to see his first real friend.

◄◦►

When Harry knocked on the door of the railway carriage that Saturday morning, Old Jack had clearly been waiting for him, because his usual Cox's Orange Pippin had been placed on the seat opposite. Harry picked it up, took a bite and sat down.

'Thank you, Mr Tar,' Harry said as he wiped some juice from his chin. He never asked where the apples came from; it just added to the mystery of the great man.

How different he was from Uncle Stan, who repeated the little he knew again and again, whereas Old Jack introduced Harry to new words, new experiences, even new worlds every week. He often wondered why Mr Tar wasn't a schoolmaster – he seemed to know even more than Miss Monday, and almost as much as Mr Holcombe. Harry was convinced that Mr Holcombe knew everything, because he never failed to answer any question Harry put to him. Old Jack smiled across at him, but didn't speak until Harry had finished his apple and thrown the core out of the window.

'What have you learnt at school this week,' the old man asked, 'that you didn't know a week ago?'

'Mr Holcombe told me there are other countries

beyond the sea that are part of the British Empire, and they are all reigned over by the King.'

'He's quite right,' said Old Jack. 'Can you name any of those countries?'

'Australia. Canada. India.' He hesitated. 'And America.'

'No, not America,' said Old Jack. 'That used to be the case, but it isn't any more, thanks to a weak Prime Minister and a sick King.'

'Who was the King, and who was the Prime Minister?' demanded Harry angrily.

'King George III was on the throne in 1776,' said Old Jack, 'but to be fair, he was a sick man, while Lord North, his Prime Minister, simply ignored what was taking place in the colonies, and, sadly, in the end our own kith and kin took up arms against us.'

'But we must have beaten them?' said Harry.

'No, we didn't,' said Old Jack. 'Not only did they have right on their side – not that that's a prerequisite for victory—'

'What does prerequisite mean?'

'Required as a pre-condition,' said Old Jack, who then continued as if he hadn't been interrupted. 'But they were also led by a brilliant general.'

'What was his name?'

'George Washington.'

'You told me last week that Washington was the capital of America. Was he named after the city?'

'No, the city was named after him. It was built on an area of marshland known as Columbia, through which the Potomac River flows.'

'Is Bristol named after a man too?'

'No,' chuckled Old Jack, amused by how quickly Harry's inquisitive mind could switch from subject to subject. 'Bristol was originally called Brigstowe, which means the site of a bridge.'

'So when did it become Bristol?'

'Historians differ in their opinions,' said Old Jack, 'although Bristol Castle was built by Robert of Gloucester in 1109, when he saw the opportunity to trade wool with the Irish. After that, the city developed into a trading port. Since then it's been a centre of shipbuilding for hundreds of years, and grew even more quickly when the navy needed to expand in 1914.'

'My dad fought in the Great War,' said Harry with pride. 'Did you?'

For the first time, Old Jack hesitated before answering one of Harry's questions. He just sat there, not saying a word. 'I'm sorry, Mr Tar,' said Harry. 'I didn't mean to pry.'

'No, no,' said Old Jack. 'It's just that I haven't been asked that question for some years.' Without another word, he opened his hand to reveal a sixpence.

Harry took the little silver coin and bit it, something he'd seen his uncle do. 'Thank you,' he said before pocketing it.

'Go and buy yourself some fish and chip
dockside café, but don't tell your uncle, because
ask where you got the money.'

In truth, Harry had never told his uncle an, ...ng
about Old Jack. He'd once heard Stan tell his mum, 'The
loony ought to be locked up.' He'd asked Miss Monday
what a loony was, because he couldn't find the word in the
dictionary, and when she told him, he realized for the first
time just how stupid his Uncle Stan must be.

'Not necessarily stupid,' Miss Monday counselled,
'simply ill-informed and therefore prejudiced. I have no
doubt, Harry,' she added, 'that you'll meet many more
such men during your lifetime, some of them in far more
exalted positions than your uncle.'

3

MAISIE WAITED UNTIL she heard the front door slam
and was confident that Stan was on his way to work before
she announced, 'I've been offered a job as a waitress at the
Royal Hotel.'

No one seated round the table responded, as conversations at breakfast were supposed to follow a regular
pattern and not take anyone by surprise. Harry had a
dozen questions he wanted to ask but waited for his
grandma to speak first. She simply busied herself with

pouring another cup of tea, as if she hadn't heard her daughter in the first place.

'Will someone please say something?' said Maisie.

'I didn't even realize you were looking for another job,' ventured Harry.

'I wasn't,' said Maisie. 'But last week a Mr Frampton, the manager of the Royal, dropped into Tilly's for coffee. He came back several times, and then he offered me a job!'

'I thought you were happy at the tea shop,' said Grandma, finally joining in. 'After all, Miss Tilly pays well, and the hours suit.'

'I am happy,' said Harry's mum, 'but Mr Frampton's offering me five pounds a week, and half of all the tips. I could be bringing home as much as six pounds on a Friday.' Grandma sat there with her mouth wide open.

'Will you have to work nights?' asked Harry, once he'd finished licking Stan's porridge bowl.

'No, I won't,' Maisie said, ruffling her son's hair, 'and what's more I'll get one day off a fortnight.'

'Are your clothes posh enough for a grand hotel like the Royal?' asked Grandma.

'I'll be supplied with a uniform, and a fresh white apron every morning. The hotel even has its own laundry.'

'I don't doubt it,' said Grandma, 'but I can think of one problem we're all going to have to learn to live with.'

'And what's that, Mum?' asked Maisie.

'You could end up earnin' more than Stan, and he's not going to like that, not one little bit.'

'Then he'll just have to learn to live with it, won't he?' said Grandpa, offering an opinion for the first time in weeks.

—◇—

The extra money was going to come in useful, especially after what had happened at the Holy Nativity. Maisie had been about to leave the church after the service when Miss Monday walked purposefully down the aisle towards her.

'Can I have a private word with you, Mrs Clifton?' she asked, before turning and walking back down the aisle towards the vestry. Maisie chased after her like a child in the Pied Piper's wake. She feared the worst. What had Harry been up to this time?

Maisie followed the choir mistress into the vestry and felt her legs give way when she saw the Reverend Watts, Mr Holcombe and another gentleman standing there. As Miss Monday closed the door quietly behind her, Maisie began to shake uncontrollably.

The Reverend Watts placed an arm around her shoulder. 'There's nothing for you to worry about, my dear,' he assured her. 'On the contrary, I hope you will feel we are the bearers of glad tidings,' he added, offering her a seat. Maisie sat down, but still couldn't stop shaking.

Once everyone was seated, Miss Monday took over. 'We wanted to talk to you about Harry, Mrs Clifton,' she began. Maisie pursed her lips; what could the boy possibly have done to bring three such important people together?

'I'll not beat about the bush,' the choir mistress continued. 'The music master at St Bede's has approached me and asked if Harry would consider entering his name for one of their choral scholarships.'

'But he's very happy at Holy Nativity,' said Maisie. 'In any case, where is St Bede's Church? I've never even heard of it.'

'St Bede's is not a church,' said Miss Monday. 'It's a choir school that supplies choristers for St Mary Redcliffe, which was famously described by Queen Elizabeth as the fairest and godliest church in all the land.'

'So would he have to leave his school, as well as the church?' asked Maisie in disbelief.

'Try to look upon it as an opportunity that might change his whole life, Mrs Clifton,' said Mr Holcombe, speaking for the first time.

'But wouldn't he have to mix with posh, clever boys?'

'I doubt if there will be many children at St Bede's cleverer than Harry,' said Mr Holcombe. 'He's the brightest lad I've ever taught. Although we get the occasional boy into the grammar school, none of our pupils has ever been offered the chance of a place at St Bede's before.'

'There's something else you need to know before you make up your mind,' said the Reverend Watts. Maisie looked even more anxious. 'Harry would have to leave home during term time, because St Bede's is a boarding school.'

'Then it's out of the question,' said Maisie. 'I couldn't afford it.'

'That shouldn't prove a problem,' said Miss Monday. 'If Harry is offered a scholarship, the school would not only waive any fees, but also award him a bursary of ten pounds a term.'

'But is this one of those schools where the fathers wear suits and ties, and the mothers don't work?' asked Maisie.

'It's worse than that,' said Miss Monday, trying to make light of it. 'The masters wear long black gowns and mortarboards on their heads.'

'Still,' said the Reverend Watts joining in, 'at least there would be no more leatherings for Harry. They're far more refined at St Bede's. They just cane the boys.'

Only Maisie didn't laugh. 'But why would he want to leave home?' she asked. 'He's settled at Merrywood Elementary, and he won't want to give up being senior chorister at Holy Nativity.'

'I must confess that my loss would be even greater than his,' said Miss Monday. 'But then, I'm sure our Lord would not want me to stand in the way of such a gifted child, simply because of my own selfish desires,' she added quietly.

'Even if I agree,' said Maisie, playing her last card, 'that doesn't mean Harry will.'

'I had a word with the boy last week,' admitted Mr

Holcombe. 'Of course he was apprehensive about such a challenge, but if I recall, his exact words were "I'd like to have a go, sir, but only if you think I'm good enough." But,' he added before Maisie could respond, 'he also made it clear that he wouldn't even consider the idea unless his mother agreed.'

◄◦►

Harry was both terrified and excited by the thought of taking the entrance exam, but just as anxious about failing and letting so many people down as he was about succeeding and having to leave home.

During the following term, he never once missed a lesson at Merrywood, and when he returned home each evening, he went straight up to the bedroom he shared with Uncle Stan, where, with the aid of a candle, he studied for hours that until then he hadn't realized existed. There were even occasions when his mother found Harry sound asleep on the floor, open books scattered around him.

Every Saturday morning he continued to visit Old Jack, who seemed to know a great deal about St Bede's, and continued to teach Harry about so many other things, almost as if he knew where Mr Holcombe had left off.

On Saturday afternoons, much to the disgust of Uncle Stan, Harry no longer accompanied him to Ashton Gate to watch Bristol City, but returned to Merrywood, where Mr Holcombe gave him extra lessons. It would be years before Harry worked out that Mr Holcombe was also for-going his regular visits to support the Robins, in order to teach him.

As the day of the examination drew nearer, Harry became even more frightened of failure than of the possi-bility of success.

On the appointed day, Mr Holcombe accompanied his star pupil to the Colston Hall, where the two-hour exam-ination would take place. He left Harry at the entrance to the building, with the words, 'Don't forget to read each question twice before you even pick up your pen,' a piece of advice he'd repeated several times during the past week. Harry smiled nervously, and shook hands with Mr Holcombe as if they were old friends.

He entered the examination hall to find about sixty other boys standing around in small groups, chattering. It was clear to Harry that many of them already knew each other, while he didn't know anyone. Despite this, one or two of them stopped talking and glanced at him as he made his way to the front of the hall trying to look confi-dent.

'Abbott, Barrington, Cabot, Clifton, Deakins, Fry . . .'

Harry took his place at a desk in the front row, and just moments before the clock struck ten, several masters in long black gowns and mortarboards swept in and placed examination papers on the desks in front of each candi-date.

'Gentlemen,' said a master standing at the front of the hall, who had not taken part in the distribution of the papers, 'my name is Mr Frobisher, and I am your invigilator. You have two hours in which to answer one hundred questions. Good luck.'

A clock he couldn't see struck ten. All around him, pens dipped into inkwells and began to scratch furiously across paper, but Harry simply folded his arms, leant on the desk and read each question slowly. He was among the last to pick up his pen.

Harry couldn't know that Mr Holcombe was pacing up and down on the pavement outside, feeling far more nervous than his pupil. Or that his mother was glancing up at the clock in the foyer of the Royal Hotel every few minutes as she served morning coffee. Or that Miss Monday was kneeling in silent prayer before the altar at Holy Nativity.

Moments after the clock had struck twelve, the examination papers were gathered up and the boys were allowed to leave the hall, some laughing, some frowning, others thoughtful.

When Mr Holcombe first saw Harry, his heart sank. 'Was it that bad?' he asked.

Harry didn't reply until he was certain no other boy could overhear his words. 'Not at all what I expected,' he said.

'What do you mean?' asked Mr Holcombe anxiously.

'The questions were far too easy,' replied Harry.

Mr Holcombe felt that he had never been paid a greater compliment in his life.

─◄○►─

'Two suits, madam, grey. One blazer, navy. Five shirts, white. Five stiff collars, white. Six pairs of calf-length socks, grey. Six sets of undergarments, white. And one St Bede's tie.' The shop assistant checked the list carefully. 'I think that covers everything. Oh, no, the boy will also need a school cap.' He reached under the counter, opened a drawer and removed a red and black cap which he placed on Harry's head. 'A perfect fit,' he pronounced. Maisie smiled at her son with considerable pride. Harry looked every inch a St Bede's boy. 'That will be three pounds, ten shillings and six pence, madam.'

Maisie tried not to look too dismayed. 'Is it possible to purchase any of these items second-hand?' she whispered.

'No, madam, this is not a second-hand shop,' said the assistant, who had already decided that this customer would not be allowed to open an account.

Maisie opened her purse, handed over four pound notes and waited for the change. She was relieved that St Bede's had paid the first term's bursary in advance, especially as she still needed to buy two pairs of leather shoes, black with laces, two pairs of gym shoes, white with laces, and one pair of slippers, bedroom.

The assistant coughed. 'The boy will also need two pairs of pyjamas and a dressing gown.'

'Yes, of course,' said Maisie, hoping she had enough money left in her purse to cover the cost.

'And am I to understand that the boy is a choral scholar?' asked the assistant, looking more closely at his list.

'Yes, he is,' Maisie replied proudly.

'Then he'll also require one cassock, red, two surplices, white, and a St Bede's medallion.' Maisie wanted to run out of the shop. 'Those items will be supplied by the school when he attends his first choir practice,' the assistant added before handing over her change. 'Will you be requiring anything else, madam?'

'No, thank you,' said Harry, who picked up the two bags, grabbed his mother by the arm and led her quickly out of T.C. Marsh, Tailors of Distinction.

—◦—

Harry spent the Saturday morning before he was due to report to St Bede's with Old Jack.

'Are you nervous about going to a new school?' asked Old Jack.

'No, I'm not,' said Harry defiantly. Old Jack smiled. 'I'm terrified,' he admitted.

'So is every new bug, as you'll be called. Try to treat the whole thing as if you're starting out on an adventure to a new world, where everyone begins as equals.'

'But the moment they hear me speak, they'll realize I'm not their equal.'

'Possibly, but the moment they hear you sing, they'll realize they're not *your* equal.'

'Most of them will have come from rich families, with servants.'

'That will only be a consolation for the more stupid ones,' said Old Jack.

'And some of them will have brothers at the school, and even fathers and grandfathers who were there before them.'

'Your father was a fine man,' said Old Jack, 'and none of them will have a better mother, of that I can assure you.'

'You knew my father?' said Harry, unable to mask his surprise.

'Knew would be an exaggeration,' said Old Jack, 'but I observed him from afar, as I have many others who have worked at the docks. He was a decent, courageous, God-fearing man.'

'But do you know how he died?' asked Harry, looking Old Jack in the eye, hoping he would at last get an honest reply to the question that had troubled him for so long.

'What have you been told?' asked Old Jack cautiously.

'That he was killed in the Great War. But as I was born in 1920, even I can work out that that can't be possible.'

Old Jack didn't speak for some time. Harry remained on the edge of his seat.

'He was certainly badly wounded in the war, but you're right, that was not the cause of his death.'

'Then how did he die?' asked Harry.

'If I knew, I'd tell you,' replied Old Jack. 'But there were so many rumours flying around at the time that I wasn't sure who to believe. However, there are several men, and three in particular, who undoubtedly know the truth about what happened that night.'

'My uncle Stan must be one of them,' said Harry, 'but who are the other two?'

Old Jack hesitated, before he replied, 'Phil Haskins and Mr Hugo.'

'Mr Haskins? The ganger?' said Harry. 'He wouldn't give me the time of day. And who's Mr Hugo?'

'Hugo Barrington, the son of Sir Walter Barrington.'

'The family who own the shipping line?'

'The same,' replied Old Jack, fearing he'd gone too far.

'And are they also decent, courageous, God-fearing men?'

'Sir Walter is among the finest men I've ever known.'

'But what about his son, Mr Hugo?'

'Not cut from the same cloth, I fear,' said Old Jack, without further explanation.

We hope you enjoyed this extract from

ONLY TIME WILL TELL

*All seven titles in this brilliant series are available
to buy now in paperback and ebook*

HALF PRICE OFF ANY BOOK IN
THE CLIFTON CHRONICLES
WITH THIS VOUCHER IN WHSMITH